BUENOS AIRES NOIR

EDITED BY ERNESTO MALLO

Translated by John Washington & M. Cristina Lambert

BROOKLYN, NEW YORK, USA
BALLYDEHOB, CO. CORK, IRELAND

This collection is comprised of works of fiction. All names, charaters, places, and incidents are the product of the authors' imaginations. Any resemblance to real events or persons, living or dead, is entirely coincidental.

Published by Akashic Books
©2017 Akashic Books

Series concept by Tim McLoughlin and Johnny Temple
Buenos Aires map by Sohrab Habibion

ISBN: 978-1-61775-522-4
Library of Congress Control Number: 2017936216

Printed in Canada

Akashic Books
Brooklyn, New York, USA
Ballydehob, Co. Cork, Ireland
Twitter: @AkashicBooks
Facebook: AkashicBooks
E-mail: info@akashicbooks.com
Website: www.akashicbooks.com

ALSO IN THE AKASHIC NOIR SERIES

BUENOS AIRES

9

4

8

201

7

MONTE CASTRO

MATADEROS

RÍO DE LA PLATA

Núñez

Belgrano R

Palermo

Barrio Parque

Chacarita

Recoleta

Parque Chas

Bario II

Almagro

Balvanera

Caballito

San Telmo

Matanza River

TABLE OF CONTENTS

INTRODUCTION
ON THE EDGE OF CHAOS

Translated by John Washington & John Granger

B uenos Aires is such an improbable city that it had to be founded twice. The first time, Pedro de Mendoza invested all the money he had stolen during the sacking of Rome to mount an extravagant expedition. He had hoped to discover a plant, supposedly growing in the Indies, that could cure his syphilis. The crusade was a disaster, thwarted by Alonso de Cabrera, who sold all their provisions to the highest bidder. When the settlers felt hunger, and the Querandí natives tightened a noose around their necks, they started supplementing their diet with boots, belts, and even some of their companions. Many of the two thousand men in that first expedition went on to other destinies; the two hundred or so who remained—and somehow survived the horrible conditions—had to be rescued.

Later, to defend against pirates, the city was founded again as a fort and a customs office that imposed tight restrictions on trade as riches from the Potosí silver mine were whisked away on La Plata River. The inhabitants of the new Buenos Aires watched as boats loaded with slaves captured in West Africa sailed up the muddy water on the way to the mines, and boats loaded down with silver and other precious metals sailed back downriver from Potosí. The commerce immediately attracted smugglers, and in just a few years, Buenos Aires was supporting a robust illegal market with the usual crimes and criminals that accompany the endeavors of smugglers and city officials. The city soon overtook both Asunción and Lima in economic and strategic importance.

These shaky and troubled beginnings have left their marks on the character and temperament of Buenos Aires. Its inhabitants display the mischief found on the edges of the law, the rush of a passing reflection, and a surprising capacity to adapt to new situations.

The distinctive music of the city is the tango, the sensual dance par excellence—originally from the Candombe dance of African slaves, and later developed in brothels and bordellos. It is sex turned into song.

Like all great cities, Buenos Aires is no stranger to unpredictable and disordered spurts of immigration, with people from all over the world coming in search of a better life, mixing in with the locals into the underground hierarchy: from the stickup man to the bank robber, from the drug trafficker to the white-collar swindler. Here the *señorones* live with the peons, the crème with the riffraff. The city is, as Enrique Santos Discépolo's tango describes, an antique stall with jumbled piles of old and forgotten objects.

Stravinsky and Don Bosco
hand in hand with La Mignon,
Don Chico and Napoleon,
Carnera and San Martín.
As through the dirty windows
of the pawnshops:
life itself, jumbled,
and the Bible that cries
on the hook beside the boiler . . .

Buenos Aires: city of contrasts, contradictions; always on the edge of chaos; in love with its own disorder despite the crude, transitory violence, the lack of law and order, the ubiquitously hurled insult, the thunderous boom of traffic, and honking, hurled curses. Its inhabitants love/hate the city. In the language of the port-dwellers, irony is currency. The multimillionaires of Puerto Madero deal in this irony as fluently as the workers in the "misery cities," which is what we call the poorest neighborhoods in Buenos Aires. This shared language comes from the mansions and the shanties that are built side by side, separated by nothing but a single street or railroad track—contradiction within eyesight.

In the stories that make up this volume we glimpse what Buenos Aires really is: distinctive points of view, as well as the narrative potential of a city that has reinvented itself many times over. This collection highlights the relations between the social and economic classes—from their tensions, from their cruelties, and also from their love. Deep inside, inhabitants of Buenos Aires live this contradiction.

André Malraux called Buenos Aires the capital of an empire that never existed. This empire, which never existed historically, which was never a conquering force or a military or economic powerhouse, exists in the strength of its literature, born of necessity—born of the precarious nature of its politics and economy—and born of its irreverent capacity to survive.

Ernesto Mallo
Buenos Aires, Argentina
August 2017

PART I

How to Get Away With . . .

THE DEAD WIFE

BY INÉS GARLAND
Belgrano R

Translated by John Washington

He told me that the green iron door that opened up to Superí Street would creak, that the big wooden door was jammed and that the hall would be dark and that I should leave the keys in a blue ceramic dish on the mahogany dresser against the wall. Then, he told me, I'd have to cross the living room to get to the garden, but little did I know—and never would I have imagined—that upon entering that house for the first time, despite all the instructions he had given me, I was crossing, irrevocably, the threshold of the world I knew and entering into another one.

They were in the garden. Through the back window I could see them before they could see me. Pablo was talking with a glass of white wine in his hand, while his two children looked at him from across the table. His daughter had her elbows on the white tablecloth, and his son was reclined back in his chair, legs extended and crossed at the ankles. They were in the shade of a tall oak tree, and all around them, like the sea, the garden glimmered. They didn't know that I had arrived, though Pablo must have been listening for my arrival. What had he told them about me? How did he explain us? That I was a friend, of course, who was going to spend the weekend with them. But how did he account for me spending the *whole* weekend with them? Because I lived in a tiny apartment in San Telmo? Because I was a lonely woman? Something that would make them feel generous, something that they could believe—he thought they were unable to take any more pain. I was going to have to go out into the courtyard, I was going to have to greet them, pretend that I barely knew anything about them, give Pablo, as if we shared nothing but a passing professional relationship, a formal kiss on the cheek. I was going to have to lie. To lie day after day, from morning until night. I wasn't ready to walk out there. So why had I agreed to come? Because I was like a slow-moving ship, and once I got going I couldn't turn without advance notice. Because my love for Pablo shook me to my bones, and he wasn't the type of man who was easy to refuse. It took me a long time to realize that I hadn't been able to deny his invitation because—however confusedly, almost unconsciously—I felt that it was my responsibility to be there, to mourn with them, to be a witness to their loss.

Pablo's wife had been sick for less than a year. Until the very end she was convinced that she was going to recover. Ten days before she died, when she could barely stand up by herself and he had to carry her to the bathroom, he had found her in the garage, crouched down and tinkering with a bicycle pedal. He told me these stories in bed, after making love. He called her sometimes when we were together, and they fought on the phone about her nurse. His wife didn't like the nurse, but Pablo didn't want to fire her. They yelled at each other, or actually only he yelled; she was too weak to yell.

"It won't do you any good to cry," he told her one night when we were walking to the theater. "Esther is staying no matter how much you scream and cry."

It was the only time that I actually said something. I told him that he shouldn't make her cry either, and the word *either* lingered and wobbled in my head. What really made her cry was so enormous that the word *either* seemed entirely out of place. But I didn't elaborate. I didn't want to know the details of their discussion. I didn't know why we were going to the theater, why I was with him, why I was witness to this fight in which Pablo's voice had an edge to it that stung, as if it was me he was speaking to. Later, when he grabbed my hand during the play, I searched his face for a leftover sign of anger. I knew that he didn't like it when he was contradicted, but his anger had seemed disproportionate to the situation, seemed to come from somewhere else, escaping in spite of his efforts. I didn't think about this fight again until the afternoon when I found out who Esther really was.

Pablo's kids didn't seem surprised when I walked out. The boy even stood to greet me, though it seemed to take a super-human will to raise his sprawled-out body. Pablo served me wine, and without hesitation they included me in their conversation. They were talking about people I didn't know, Pablo taking the time to explain: the marriages among his children's friends. I can't trace out how they ended up talking about their dead mother. I could probably say something vague like *one thing led to another*, but I think she was present the whole time, and finally someone—was it Pablo?—mentioned something that sparked the kids to start telling me anecdotes about their mother. Their anger unsettled me. But what did I know, I who still hadn't suffered any loss, about the labryinths of pain.

The boy told a story about when his mother tied his left arm to his body so that he would be forced to write with his right hand. None of them were familiar with the expression *converted lefty*. As if it were some sort of little quirk of his mother, he told about how she forced him to do his homework with his left hand tied behind his back while his sister and cousins were outside bouncing on the trampoline. His resentment was lightly masked, but in that resentment, or beneath it, there was, without knowing why, a pain that I felt almost as my own. The three of them were laughing, but I felt mournful until nightfall. Their mother was gone. She wasn't nice to her children, the reasons didn't matter.

That night, in the room they assigned to me at the end of a hallway on the first floor, thinking of her kept me awake. I had seen her only once, in the street. I'd recognized her from the photos in Pablo's office. She was tall and blond, with hair that seemed to trap the light of the sun. One of those women that people turn around to take another look at. She seemed distracted. Pablo had told me she didn't like that people walked around on the streets with headphones on. And though I was somebody who listened to music in the streets, I felt I was more aware of my surroundings than she was. She looked angry. She was still healthy, or at least, at that point, she didn't know that she was sick.

Lying there in the darkness, I listened to the noises of the house, the creaking of wood, a shutter flapping somewhere, the steps of someone who must have gone—as the noise stopped—to close the shutter. The room smelled of wood, and I could hear the sounds of cars passing outside on Superí Street, the bell of a distant train station, and the train, moments later, passing over the bridge. The image of her crouched down in the garage to fix a bicycle pedal wouldn't leave my mind. Pablo had told me that she weighed less than ninety pounds at that point. My friends had tried to convince me not to see him in those months, but he told me that he couldn't weather it, that was how he said it, that he couldn't *weather the storm* without me, and so I stayed by his side. I even fantasized about visiting her, that she would leave me her husband and children like an inheritance. She had almost twenty years on me, and she was dying. She hated me. Pablo told me so when I asked about her.

I was drifting off to sleep when the door opened and someone walked into the room and then, very carefully, closed the door. I sat up in bed and switched on the light. Pablo reached and turned it off and then put his hand over my mouth. He had an urgency to him that I didn't recognize. He kissed me, violently, lay down on top of me, and pinned my arms down. His legs pushed themselves between my own and, without giving me time to undress, he entered me and began to thrust, his insteps pushing against the soles of my feet. After finishing he jumped up like a cat and, running his fingers into my hair, made a fist and kissed me again, a hard kiss, almost knocking into my teeth.

"See you tomorrow," he whispered. And then he left.

I felt along the walls of the hallway toward the bathroom. My body was in shock; I needed a moment to regain my equilibrium. On the way to the bathroom, I could hear somebody sobbing behind one of the closed bedroom doors.

That week I was offered a new job in an English bookstore on the corner of Conde and Echeverría, just three blocks from Pablo's house. I needed to stop working with Pablo, and I'd cast out so many lines to so many people that I was never able to track down who had landed the job for me. The person who interviewed me couldn't even tell me. The commute from San Telmo was long, but I needed the work, and selling books sounded wonderful. I already knew the bookstore and loved its particular smell—of soap, paper, and wood—and loved its English art books, cookbooks, baby books, the islands with towers of novels, and the shelves of poetry. Lydia, my work partner, kindly took me under her wing, showing me the ropes, the quirks of the place, everything I needed to know to get started. The rest I'd learn as the days ran by.

My first customer was a woman dressed in blue hospital scrubs and tennis shoes. There was something fierce in her eyes; she had strong hands and a hard, sensual face. If I'd had more experience as a bookseller I would have been able to recognize that this woman wasn't going to buy anything. She asked lots of questions, but mostly just stared at me. I thought I was imagining things, though, after she'd left, Lydia confirmed my suspicions.

"She's a strange woman," she explained. "Lives across the street but she never bought a book here. I don't even think she speaks English."

Lydia's parents were from England, and I thought her comment sounded a little snobby, but it was true that the woman had referred to books only by pointing, or pulling one off the shelf—never speaking a single word of English.

"Maybe she's more interested in you than in the books," Lydia said.

This thought didn't make it any easier for me, especially when the woman started coming in on a daily basis. Sometimes she came in the morning, other times in the afternoon, just before closing. She didn't buy anything, but she made laps in the aisles, taking books off the shelves and then stashing them wherever she happened to be. I always had the impression that she was watching me. One afternoon she stood outside in front of the store for almost an hour, talking on the phone and looking in through the window, shifting her weight from one foot to the other, laughing, playing with her hair, letting it fall to her neck, where it would lightly caress the line of her clavicle that peeked out just above the collar of her scrubs. There was something so sensual in her movements. From inside the store I couldn't tell where she was looking exactly, but without really knowing why, I tried to avoid her gaze.

"When you hide, she looks for you," Lydia told me.

That was the day we started calling her *the nurse*. Sometimes, when I was working in the back, Lydia would pop in to say that the nurse had come in to toy with me, and I'd stay out of sight until I knew she was gone. I'd see her coming and going from the building across the street at random hours, and Lydia, who would occasionally take a break at the tea house on the same block, would see her sitting at one of the sidewalk tables or, if it was raining, sitting inside and talking on the phone, with a teapot in front of her. She always seemed to be on her phone.

Pablo also started to stop by every day, at random hours. He'd buy books so the boss wouldn't suspect anything, but he'd also do things that made me uncomfortable. He'd come up behind me when I was checking the price of a book he'd asked about and he'd lean against me, taking advantage of the islands of books that would conceal us from the waist down. He'd grab me by the hips, or would put a hand between my legs or, if we were standing in some back aisle, he'd force them apart and caress me, while pretending to scan book titles. I struggled between feeling aroused and feeling appalled. I liked Pablo a lot; he blinded me, just like a deer is blinded by the headlights of an oncoming car.

One afternoon in the bookstore, Pablo came up behind me and cornered me against the storefront window, pretending to ask something about an art book, when the nurse appeared on the other side of the glass. Although I couldn't see Pablo's face behind me, I had the impression that he and the nurse were looking at each other. He cupped his hand between my legs and started to rub against me. I pushed away from him. It was only a moment, but I lost my breath.

"What was that?" Lydia asked me after Pablo left with a gift-wrapped copy of Annemarie Heinrich's book of nudes, which cost a fortune.

"Must be a gift for someone important," I said.

"Don't play stupid," Lydia responded.

But I couldn't answer.

That weekend Pablo invited me to his house again. It had been two months since that first weekend visit. This time his kids weren't home, and he had planned a dinner with a few couples he hadn't seen in a while. It all seemed too fast for me—only six months ago these people had lost their friend. But Pablo didn't hear my objections. I helped him cook a curry with a mountain of ingredients that we had to chop and sort on the counter before even starting; we also delicately laid out a cheese plate with an attention to detail bordering on obsession. Everything had to be perfect, and, as the hour approached, he kept finding more and more indispensable little chores we had to do—all of it making me more and more nervous.

I had heard the names of his friends very often and knew so much about them that the predicament they were in was immeasurable. They asked me a bunch of questions, but sometimes gave each other looks, or talked about things I didn't understand. Pablo was even worse, and it seemed that they were all looking down on me, as if I were a prized pet. As the night wore on, however, and with the help of bottle after bottle of wine that Pablo opened, they started warming up to me, and at nearly two in the morning one of the women, Delia, asked me to join her on the patio for a cigarette. As soon as we sat down she began swinging on the white iron chairs and talked about Pablo's dead wife. It wasn't what I was expecting. She told me how beautiful the woman was.

"Traffic would stop to stare at her."

And then she dove into a story which I had trouble following at first. The setting was in the country, summertime. Pablo's wife was dressed in white pants.

"Perfectly white pants, tight, super-tight, so tight there was no part of her left to the imagination," Delia said in a slow, bogged-down voice.

Pablo was flying to New York the next day; his wife, knowing he had lovers in some of the cities he traveled to, didn't want him to go.

"She was drunk," Delia said, raising her own glass. "No pain. There were four or five men in my house that weekend. They hovered around her like bumblebees.

"Pablo's wife was playing backgammon with the men. She'd already beaten two of them. And then it started raining. A torrential rain. Like the sky itself was dropping. The daughter came in, but the little boy, still practically a baby, stayed out in the rain. And there she was, in the middle of the scene: radiant, gorgeous, the men eating out of her hand. Pablo was sick with jealousy. You don't know what this woman was like. How brazen she was. Her daughter was right next to her and she didn't even look at her. I didn't do anything, it wasn't my place, but finally I had to go and look for the little boy. He was sitting in the middle of the garden, soaking wet, and if I hadn't gone out he would have stayed there in the rain because all she cared about was that Pablo was going to New York and she would have her revenge."

Delia finished her champagne. From the house we heard

the laughter of the men, of Pablo. Delia made a gesture of contempt and said, "You're very young to be playing with Pablo. Why are you with him? Did he ever introduce you to Esther?"

I wanted her to tell me more, everything she knew. The dew had dropped against my cold skin, shimmering against the white iron of the armrests, beading on the glass of the tabletop.

"Pour me more champagne," Delia said.

And in the blink of an eye, she cut the curiosity that tethered me to her.

The world can synchronize sometimes, things develop on their own, and then bump into each other, synthesize. Considered with some perspective, everything always points to its own completion. Would something have changed if I had asked Pablo questions that night? He probably would have lied to me, and I would heave trod that same path, slowly approaching the inevitable. I decided to look at only one side of things, take the most convenient path. Delia was an unattractive woman. She saw the world through her own ugliness. What motivated her was a sick jealousy for the dead woman, developed over years of envy, years of looking at something totally out of her reach. She exaggerated and, because she'd never been looked at like that, pointed her finger at her dead friend. She, too, had been blinded by Pablo and his wife, by the intensity that drove them, indifferent to anything that didn't reflect back on themselves. What would happen later doesn't erase this partial truth.

That weekend felt like a fruit ripening in the sun. Pablo and I spent all morning in bed, and in the afternoon we walked around the neighborhood. On Melián Street we took photos of the Tipuanas under the free light of their huge tops; we toured around, snapping photos of sculptures of stone faces in front of houses, starting with the one over the entrance to the bookstore. We walked hand in hand, inhaling the scents of the local gardens, trying to remember the names of the flowers and trees. Approaching the central plaza, we stopped under orange trees growing over the wall of the Hirsch Palace, and Pablo pulled off a blossom. I buried my nose in the palm of his hand to smell. From the plaza came the sound of drums.

"Carnival," Pablo said.

We entered into the crowds, even dancing a little. Happiness. To really feel it, everybody else has to be out of the picture. I've always been good at making that happen.

I could say that what really set everything off was Esther herself. But it's not that simple. One Monday before we were closing up at the bookstore, the nurse forgot her wallet, or maybe purposefully left it behind. Lydia found it.

"Your nurse's name is Esther Villar," Lydia told me, showing me the open wallet. It felt like a wave of violence was approaching, but I could only see it out of the corner of my eye.

I called the number that I found on a card in the wallet, stuck behind a plastic window. Esther asked me to stop by, and I told her I would. I crossed the street. Entered the building. Took the elevator. Found the door open and heard Esther yell for me to come in.

"Be with you in a second," she called from a room at the end of the hall to the left of the front door.

I stood there. A small library, some strange glass bookcase with an old globe on top of it. On the first shelf, as if it were waiting there for me, sticking out almost obscenely, was the Annemarie Heinrich book of nudes. I left the wallet right next to it on the shelf and I walked back out the door.

* * *

I waited an hour at the train station for Pablo. The train doors opened and the people streamed out, passing right by me, talking on their phones, carrying their suitcases, their backpacks, tall people, short people, good people, bad people, whole lives, people in a rush, people with the night awaiting them, with empty houses or full houses, with their lovers or their fears or their loneliness waiting for them. Men. Some of them looked at me. Others didn't. None of them were Pablo. The trains weren't spitting out Pablo. Yet I knew what train he was arriving on. I knew it before I even saw him walking toward me amongst the throng of people, before he smiled, before my face erased that smile. I jumped back when he tried to hug me.

"Who's Esther?"

I shouldn't have taken even another step with him. But I wanted to know. All I wanted was to know. I wanted to see with clear eyes. If I was going to walk away, I wanted to know what I was walking away from. This is what I told myself. I don't know if it was the truth.

Esther opened the door to her apartment as if she had been waiting for us, and we entered without a word. Pablo's anger reminded me of the conversation with his wife I had overheard on the way to the theater. Esther seemed just as angry. They acted as if I wasn't even there.

"This wasn't part of the deal," Pablo had to say three times before she could bring herself to respond, though it became clear that neither of them had respected whatever the deal was.

The deal. The first part of which, as I understood it, was to kill his wife. They didn't exactly say that. Instead they used the word *accelerate*. Accelerate her death. The second part of the deal, according to Esther, was tacit. According to Pablo, it was only ever in her imagination. According to Pablo, this second part of the deal had never existed.

"What was it?" Esther asked. "Was I not refined enough for you? Or is it because she's younger? I could tell the police, you know."

They continued to speak without looking at me. I hadn't left when I had the chance, but I could still leave. I knew what I had come to find out. But I didn't move because I couldn't. Pablo put his arm around Esther and pulled her toward him; at the same time, with his other hand, he grabbed me by the wrist. I could have gotten away. Both of us could have gotten away. But then he kissed her, and then he kissed me, and he pushed us together and Esther buried her face in my neck and Pablo had his hand on the small of my back and then he moved it between my legs and Esther licked my neck. Desire overtook me. I wanted to kiss him, but even though he was close, his body pushed up against the both of us, he had pulled his head back to look at us, and his mouth was too far away. He seemed angry. The anger was like another presence, a fourth person, the tie that bound Esther and me together. Esther moaned; Pablo let go of me and grabbed her neck. I could have screamed, I could have pushed him away. I don't even know what I could have done. But instead I stayed, dazzled. Esther glanced at me, and then at Pablo. I can't say if it was a look of surprise or if she'd had a revelation. She seemed to surrender; she was as dazzled as I was.

Pablo followed her body as it fell to the floor, not releasing his grip on her neck. Finally, he let go. I kneeled down. Pablo took my hand and put it against Esther's still-warm skin. There, on my knees, like an acolyte, I looked into his eyes. There was no anger left in them. And then, yes, he kissed me.

CROCHET

BY INÉS FERNÁNDEZ MORENO

Parque Chas

Translated by M. Cristina Lambert

After searching for almost two years and weathering several financial crises, we finally found the right house for our budget. It was in Parque Chas, at the corner of Constantinopla and Bucarest. A big, run-down house, but with the romantic air of a small abandoned castle. It had two floors and was surrounded by an overgrown yard presided over by two cypress trees.

"It's a chalet like the ones the English constructed when they came to build the railroads," Andrés explained.

"The yard doesn't look very English," I said, looking down-heartedly at the invasion of weeds and the remains of a chicken coop where three pygmy hens were still pecking and shitting.

"But it surrounds the whole house; you can't compare that to the pathetic idea of a garden we have now. Take lots of photos, please!"

Like a thoughtful copilot, I kept a thorough record of all our forays with my new cell phone camera.

But inside the house we continued to disagree. Where I saw the drawing room as an Etruscan grave, he saw large windows where light would stream in; where I saw a dilapidated kitchen, a creaking floor, and narrow corridors that led to dungeon-like rooms, he saw walls to knock down, a floor full of possibilities, and excellent ventilation.

And he was the architect, so I trusted his ideas. And we bought it.

The previous owner's name was Adriana Costa, and she was probably around twenty-five years old, although she was pale and withdrawn which made her look older. According to what she told us, she had lived there with her divorced mother, her grandmother, and a maiden aunt who had been a veterinarian. Unhappy women who, perhaps as a final act of dejection, had all died before their time. As they disappeared, she had limited herself to closing off their rooms, without touching a thing. Since she shared a room with her mother, she decided after her death to move to the drawing room, and she lived there amid the chaos, with clothes and shoes piled up in the corners, books and papers on the floor, and the company of three old and odoriferous dogs left by Clarisa, the veterinarian aunt who'd had up to a dozen dogs at one time. I would leave those encounters sneezing and quite depressed, but Andrés's constructive optimism was unalterable.

A few days before the agreed-upon date for the closing, we stopped by the house and found Adriana disheveled, in a bathrobe, removing buttons from a pile of old clothes.

"I haven't taken everything away yet," she told us. "I'm going to need a few more days . . ."

Since we were in a hurry and planned to do a complete renovation, we offered to help her.

"I still have to do the lower level," she told us, "especially my aunt's office; it's crammed with useless things. And the little hens . . ."

We assured her we would throw everything out. And take care of the hens.

She accepted with relief, and a few days later we began the work in earnest.

As we pulled down the dark wood paneling covering the walls and opened large windows that would face the future garden, the house began to transform itself, as if by a miracle, into what Andrés had imagined. I documented each change for our renovation scrapbook.

Six months later, we had little money left, and the completion of the work was delayed, but since most of the house was now inhabitable we decided to move in anyway.

With the excitement of the changes, we quickly got used to living in a house with two areas: the new one, bright and cheerful, and the one from the past with the veterinarian's office, the ruined laundry room, and the gloomy yard where several small brick structures stood at irregular intervals.

"They're dog graves," Pedro, the work foreman, had said. He had been told so by a neighbor, the same one who had delightedly accepted the three pygmy hens.

But the gloomiest part of the house was the veterinary office, which had a shelf with a row of animal skulls of various sizes and a basket filled with bones. Scattered about were pieces of wood, washbowls, an armchair without a seat, a collection of veterinary magazines, and several loose drawers with a random miscellany of objects.

The built-in closet in the back wasn't any better. When Andrés managed to open it with a hard pull, a frightening object fell from the top. A huge spider? An embalmed cat? I kicked it, and then cautiously approached until I saw it was an old wig, with moth-eaten hair. It made me nauseous so we decided to leave the rest of the task for another time. After that, we called the place the little room of horrors.

It was not easy to get to Constantinopla and Bucarest. I had to take the subway downtown and get off at Los Incas, the last station on the B line. Then I had to walk about ten blocks—briefly going deep into those circular little streets named after European cities—Berlin, Dublin, Londres—like someone getting lost in a dream. One corner would end in an unexpected turn, a tiny little square, or in a point converging with itself, like the corner of Bauness and Bauness.

Like in any suburban neighborhood, there were low houses with their identical little front yards and their tender details: welcome signs, ceramic ducks or dwarves, flower beds protected by a small nylon cover. But peculiarity also flourished: neighbors occupying up to half the sidewalk with their own flowerpots; a newspaper vendor who also sold eggs; a newsstand guarded by a dog; a pharmacist who read tarot cards; a greengrocer on Torrent Street who sang the praises of any vegetable or fruit one asked him for.

One afternoon when I was coming home—tired, but more open than ever to the neighborhood spirit, as I had just been granted two months of freelance work at the magazine—I stopped on Ginebra Street in front of a window lined with geraniums and crocheted curtains. Against the glass, there was a picture of Saint Expeditus and underneath, a sign offering *Crochet and Costume Jewelry Lessons*. I took several photos of it and remembered with tenderness that my grandmother used to crochet. I had never had the patience to learn. Perhaps my life in Parque Chas would now allow that deliberate and relaxing activity.

The next morning at breakfast, I told Andrés about my explorations in the neighborhood and the idea of taking crochet lessons with a neighbor. He was also making his own discoveries. He talked about the auto mechanic on Barzana Street where he'd had some spark plugs changed: his name was Giacomo and he had been a baritone.

"Now he no longer sings, but he talks nonstop. He told me he knew the Costa family well—and especially the veterinarian aunt. Apparently, she was a beautiful woman. He'd heard some stories because, besides being an old neighbor, he was the ex–police captain Padeletti's partner."

"But at some point the beauty started collecting bones," I said, remembering the basket of bones and the skulls in her office. "We should empty out that place once and for all, don't you think?"

So when Pedro came to install the missing baseboards, we asked him to start with the yard that same week, and to help us empty out the little room of horrors.

Pedro, with his calmness and his gentle accent, said we would have to burn incense afterward. His wife recommended doing that to cleanse the place. "*One must especially safeguard from the envy of the dead*, she says, *which is the worst poison.*"

Later, while having coffee in the kitchen, he told me his nephew Eladio was studying veterinary medicine, and that perhaps he might be interested in the magazines, and even the ominous dog skulls and bones. He would take them, he decided. "One man's trash is another man's treasure," he declared.

I left him working in the yard and decided to go over to the place offering crochet lessons. I went down Cádiz, and after several wrong turns came out on Ginebra, where I immediately recognized the window with the geraniums. On the stone front of the house, next to the door, was a bronze plaque that said, *Eduardo Brunner. Osteopath.* I rang the bell.

The woman who opened the door must have been over seventy but did not look at all like a knitting grandma. She was tall and robust and had high cheekbones and fiery eyes that she attempted to control. She shook my hand right away and told me her name was Franca. She led me to a living room, quite spacious, but with huge, dark furniture, around which she moved with impressive agility. Crocheted handicrafts sprouted like tumors everywhere: cushions, armrest covers, table runners, and even some flowerpots with knit covers.

"Crochet," she told me, "is one of the most efficient ways to calm the mind. Better than yoga. And it keeps your hands moving, just like making jewelry. My husband, who was an osteopath, used to always say that."

That was how I found out she was the osteopath's widow, and one of the oldest residents in Parque Chas. She had moved there as a newlywed in the forties.

We agreed I would take classes on Friday mornings and that I would start with a number five needle and some four-ply wool yarn.

When we said goodbye I saw a portrait of her deceased husband in the entrance hall. I stopped to look at it. He was an attractive man, with one of those seductive looks every woman feels is meant for her. I thought it likely that he must have had many female patients complaining of bone pain.

Franca stopped next to me. "He was a man with a lot of personality and a great gift of the gab." She said it in a subdued tone, as if it were more of a reproach than something to celebrate.

A few days later, as I was leaving for the first lesson, I ran into Pedro, who had just bought some materials for the yard.

"I have to talk to you about something, Ms. Julia," he intercepted me. Pedro seemed concerned, and I assumed it would be about money. But it wasn't. "It's about the bones I took to my nephew. They were not all dog bones," he said, and then paused, as if he were giving me the opportunity to guess what he was about to say next.

They must have been cat bones, I thought to myself.

"My nephew said there were some human bones, almost a whole hand."

"A hand?" I repeated like an idiot, trying to grasp what he was telling me.

"Odd, isn't it?" he said, as he began carrying his tools out to the yard.

"Well, perhaps they were doing comparative studies . . ."

"Maybe," replied Pedro, sounding somewhat unconvinced.

I felt uneasy with the information, and during the afternoon, while replying to some e-mails, I looked up *hand bones* on the Internet. Several X-ray images of bones appeared. Without the warmth of flesh, you could see them in all their animal rawness: cold and terrible tools for grasping. In short, said the article, the human hand has twenty-seven bones. Could the information from Pedro's nephew be trustworthy? With so many bones, large and small, he could have been mistaken.

When I later told Andrés about it, he did not think much of it. Studying and comparing bones and organs is something quite customary among medical and veterinary students.

The first crochet class was very short, less than half an hour, because Franca had nearly lost her voice. She told me in whispers that she had worked as a high school teacher for more than twenty years, and since then, because of straining her voice so much, she frequently suffered from laryngitis. But she insisted I stay, and we practiced the chain stitch, the most basic crochet stitch.

While she instructed me she also knitted—looping the wool knots with a firmness that had a hypnotic effect. But her hands were perhaps her most noticeable feature: strong

hands one could imagine handling blunter tools than a crochet needle.

"It's important to make a plan of what you first want to
crochet," she recommended before I left. "That way you'll be
more eager to learn."

I had intended to make an afghan with several color
patches. I liked the idea.

"For a twin bed afghan, you're going to need several hundred four-by-four squares."

It was a long-term project. I left there a little discouraged
with some strip chains and a shapeless little patch piece, along
with the order to practice at home.

By the following Friday another neighbor had joined the
group. Her name was Lidia, and she was forty-something.

"Julia's new in the neighborhood," Franca said, introduc-
ing me, her voice now recovered.

"Yes, I'm a few blocks from here, at the corner of Bucarest
and Constantinopla."

"Oh, I thought you'd bought one of the new apartments
on Berna," said Franca.

"No, we're diagonally across from those apartments, in a
house we're remodeling."

Franca stopped crocheting, and it seemed to me she grew
pale. "Then you must be very close to the green house, Clarisa's." Her voice sounded accusatory.

"It *was* green, now it's white," I said defensively. "And I
think Clarisa was Adriana Costa's aunt. Did you know her?"

Franca got up from her seat and was silent for a moment.
"Yes, of course I knew her," she said eventually, and stood
there hesitating as if she could not remember why she had
gotten up. She finally went to the kitchen and brought out

a tray with cookies that she set on the table next to us. "We were very close friends. But she died young. These are such sad subjects," she sighed, and went back to concentrating on her crocheting.

A tense atmosphere set in. It dissolved little by little when Lidia told us her Seville orange tree was producing fruit, and very soon she would have us taste her famous jam.

By this time, spring was arriving in Parque Chas. Jasmines were blooming; true love knots were proliferating; the corner jacaranda was producing its perennial light-blue flowers and spreading its branches toward the house as if trying to embrace it. The neighborhood people were also spreading out, washing the sidewalks with buckets of water, walking their dogs, exchanging smiles as they passed.

One Saturday morning, we finally returned to the little room of horrors. We put on work gloves and began to take the useless objects out to a dumpster.

When we removed an old, bottomless, wicker rocking chair and two lounge chairs with broken pieces, a bag that looked like cement appeared against a corner.

Pedro came into the room, took a look, and said, "It's quicklime."

"It's used as a disinfectant," said Andrés.

"If you ask me, the old woman was using it to bury the dogs. You wrap them in quicklime so they won't smell."

We threw out chipped washbowls, syringes and metallic trays, piles of folders and papers, some still lifes, unstrung rackets . . . We worked until the room was completely clear. Only the closet remained.

"I'm leaving that to you," said Andrés, concluding his participation.

I took a break, and afterward opened the closet doors wide. I was overwhelmed by a sickeningly sweet, old, moldy smell, which made me gag. I haphazardly stuffed clothes, handbags, and shoes into plastic bags, and I discovered a wooden box inlaid with what looked like mother-of-pearl. Intrigued, I took it into the kitchen. It looked like a jewelry box and was missing a leg. I tried to open it, but it was locked. Pedro, who was hanging around, took out his penknife and with the unexpected skill of a locksmith opened it with a single maneuver. I gave it a superficial look: boxes of slides, some letters and documents, a bundle of saints' pictures, a small box with a sports medal and another with a silver charm shaped like a heart. Finally, at the bottom, covered with tissue paper, was a black-and-white photo. It was the portrait of a woman, and it was signed by the photographer, *Annemarie Heinrich*. I looked at it with curiosity. It must have been young Clarisa, the veterinarian aunt who loved dogs. She had long copper-colored hair, coiffed in the fashion of the time, with waves over her forehead. She had a wide mouth with an unpleasant grin, but her eyes, in contrast, were languid, like those of a romantic heroine. She wore a pearl necklace around her neck, which was thrown back provocatively. What was this beautiful woman doing among so much junk?

I imagined Adriana would like to keep some of these family memories, but when I spoke to her, she didn't seem that excited. She was moving to the south soon, where she and her boyfriend planned to open a small hotel, and she still had millions of things to take care of. But, she said, if I did not mind, she would come by Sunday to see what it was about.

The following morning, I went out early for a walk. I had two months of freedom ahead of me. That aroused in me a summery mood, a desire to work out, take pictures, prepare exotic salads . . . I stopped at the starry-eyed greengrocer on Torrent Street to buy fruit, and there I ran into Lidia, my crochet partner.

"How are your squares?" she asked me.

"Well, at least now they're starting to look like squares."

The greengrocer interrupted to show off a bunch of parsley, "more beautiful than a bride's bouquet, ladies," and we both laughed. Inspired by Lidia's friendliness, I plucked up the courage to ask her about Franca.

"Have you known her long? She seemed to react strangely when I mentioned Clarisa."

Lidia looked up with a resigned gesture, as if all mysteries came from above, then leaned toward me and said in a low voice, "A drama of passion."

Franca and Clarisa had been close friends. Inseparable, she told me, until Clarisa began to see Brunner for some spinal cord ailment.

"He was an incorrigible womanizer, he chased her and chased her, until finally . . . Well, you can imagine."

"And then?"

Lidia looked up at the sky again. She did not know much else, except that he, after a while, had disappeared. "He made them both suffer."

"Did he run off with another woman?"

"There was talk about a Chilean patient, but he was never heard from again, as if he'd just disappeared off the face of the earth."

That night when Andrés came home, I filled him in with the latest news.

"There's something mysterious about that woman, isn't there?"

"Flaubert said it: *Anything becomes interesting if you look at it long enough.* If you want more information, I suggest you go by Giacomo's garage. You can leave him the car to have the oil changed."

It was cloudy and windy early Sunday morning, but as time passed it began to clear up. When Adriana came over, around four in the afternoon, there were no more clouds in the sky. She looked very different from the pale, unkempt girl we had met some months earlier. She had cut her hair, was dressed in very fashionable, light clothes, and her eyes shone with enthusiasm, as if by freeing herself of the house she had finally been able to begin living her real life. She was surprised by the results of the renovation, by the light streaming in through the windows, by the new spaces. For a moment it seemed her eyes clouded over, as if transfixed by some existential revelation.

We had tea while she checked the contents of the jewelry box.

"She was beautiful," Adriana said when she came to Clarisa's photo. "When I was little, I thought she was a fairy."

"She never married?"

"No, although she had many admirers. She was a stern woman. My mother was a little afraid of her. *Don't do this, don't do that. Clarisa will get angry.* I was forbidden to go into her office."

When Adriana opened the little box with the silver heart, she was surprised. She lifted the charm and looked at it in the light. "She had it on a bracelet she never took off. And suddenly one day she no longer had it. She said she'd lost it."

While Adriana finished her tea she flipped through the letters, the postcards, and other old documents, putting them back in the jewelry box in no particular order.

"I don't want to keep any of these things," she said.

"Better to let go of the past, don't you think?"

"Well, it depends," I responded.

"Neither of them, not my aunt or my mother, was happy," she said with regret. Perhaps the guilt of her incipient happiness now overwhelmed her. "I'll take the photo and the medals, and I'd like you to throw out the rest. You can keep the jewelry box, if you like."

She was getting up to leave when I asked her, "Did you ever meet Franca Brunner? I'm taking crochet lessons with her."

"Of course I met her," she replied right away. "She was Clarisa's close friend. My mother couldn't stand her. She'd say she was too possessive a friend. Too . . ." She hesitated, as if she could not find the right word, before finally concluding: "You never really get to know people, do you? Later they had a deadly falling out. They say it was a story of jealousy over her husband, the one who disappeared . . . Anyway, I was very young then."

I watched her leave in a new pickup truck, suspecting we would never see each other again.

Monday morning, Andrés left me the car to have the oil changed, and I met Giacomo. He was tall and ungainly, with a huge nose and, just as Andrés had said, a torrent of words. Together with the dreamy-eyed greengrocer they would have made an unbeatable duo. As soon as I mentioned Franca, although he was already under the car to empty the crankcase, Giacomo stuck his head out from under the chassis and in that position, like a turtle turned upside down, began to tell me what he knew.

"According to my partner Paddy, she killed Brunner out of jealousy. And then they made up the story about him running away. Paddy was seeing him about his cartilage, so they were quite friendly with each other. Look," he said, and pointed at me with a monkey wrench, "the Brunner woman reported him missing like a month after her husband's disappearance. What took her so long?"

He raised the monkey wrench up high, as if about to deal a blow. "That gave her time to maneuver. Maybe she buried him in the yard, Paddy says, although he could never prove anything. They had only checked Brunner's belongings once to see if they could find signs of his possible whereabouts."

"And did they find anything?"

"Nothing. He was declared missing, years went by, and they closed the case." Giacomo finished off the story with a long "*Ssssss*," expressing the quintessential resigned forbearance of people in Buenos Aires.

I arrived earlier than usual at Franca's for the next crochet class. I had asked her for some cuttings to transplant, and with that excuse I was able to accompany her to the backyard. She had a small but very well-tended garden, with hydrangea flower beds and dense shrubs against the walls. I observed how Franca uprooted an aloe vera cutting and another of Paraguayan jasmine. With those hands, I thought, she could very well have strangled a treacherous husband. She could easily have dug a hole and buried him.

A few minutes later Lidia arrived, as did Franca's niece, who knitted dolls, caps, and wallets. I continued with my squares. I had learned to combine two colors and handle the chain stitches and different color strips. Franca and Lidia were doing something more important—a conic screen covered with a crochet knit that they would finish off with a fringe of imitation stones. Franca had spread out on our worktable a toolbox that fascinated me: it had pliers, a mini-drill, trays with small chains, a roll of black steel, curved wires called *memory wires*, hooks, large and small rings . . .

"I only have a few accessories left now, I haven't done jewelry in a while," she said modestly. I was hypnotized by the skill with which she handled the pliers: she would insert each colored stone onto a wire, and hang it from the screen edge, then close the wire with a perfect little curl. While she did so, rapidly moving her hand up and down, I noticed the bracelet on her wrist. There it was, tinkling against the pliers: a silver heart identical to the one I had found in Clarisa's jewelry box.

I could hardly concentrate on my boring squares. I remembered Adriana's rather enigmatic words. Perhaps Franca had killed Brunner. But not for the motives of passion Padeletti had imagined.

Before I left, I got up, intending to go to the bathroom. Franca pointed to the small corridor with three doors side by side. "The first one is my room," she said, "the next one is the bathroom."

The bathroom was white and tidy, with crocheted doilies covering the toilet and bidet. There was also a coat rack with shelves and a second door that must have led to the osteopath's office. After washing my hands, moved by curiosity, I turned the door handle. The latch gave way and the door opened a few millimeters. In the darkness I thought I saw someone's shadow crouched next to a desk. I covered my mouth not to scream. The door opened a few centimeters more and with a little light I began to understand what I was looking at. The silhouette hovering over the desk was not a person: it was a demonstration skeleton. I could also see anatomy charts against the walls, a stretcher, bookshelves, and a metal filing cabinet. Everything looked intact, as if just tidied up. I had my cell phone in my pocket, so I couln't resist my habit to document everything and took several quick photos, aiming a little randomly.

I closed the door to the doctor's office trying not to make a noise. Luckily, Franca and Lidia were talking animatedly, and no one had noticed my indiscretion.

When I got home I had a slight headache and decided to take a shower to clear my head. While I sponged my arms, my elbows, my knees, I shuddered. I also had a skeleton inside. I could sense that other being, made up only of bones, parodying my daily movements.

That night, my headache was worse and I felt a little feverish, but in any case I insisted on showing Andrés my photos.

"I want you to meet your alter ego," I told him.

Andrés looked at them distractedly while clearing the table.

The skeleton had its head down to one side; it must have had a piece of its frame broken, which gave it a melancholic and resigned air. The arms hung languidly at its sides and the hands . . . Oh my god! It was missing a hand!

Andrés approached and now looked more attentively. "It's also missing ribs and both feet." And with that didactic eagerness that I admired but also abhorred, he once more expounded on his theory of "arbitrary attention," a variation of the old saying, *Everything takes on the color of the glass through which you look at it*—everyone interprets things through the filter of his or her own thoughts and obsessions.

"What if it were Brunner himself? Like in 'The Purloined Letter,'" I said. "The body that never appeared is hiding in plain sight."

"Come on, Julia, an old woman who knits doilies did away with him and stripped him down to his bare bones?"

"You should see those hands," I said.

And suddenly I thought of something else. "The quick-lime, Andrés! The bag of quicklime, remember?"

Andrés did not reply right away. "Julia, take an Advil and get some rest, please. I have to get up very early tomorrow.

That night I had a disquieting dream in which I was driving on a road full of potholes. At four in the morning I was fully awake. I searched for my cell phone in the dark and looked at the photos again. I paused on the one with more light and began to enlarge it. I discovered what looked to me like evidence. First, at the joint of the shoulder blade and the humerus, then between the crouched neck and the collar bone, and in the wrist area, joining the small bones of the hand with the ulna and the radius: those little curls of black wire, the same finishes I had seen Franca making at crochet class. I could perfectly imagine her reconstructing her husband's skeleton with the patience of a goldsmith. The hands and feet must be the most complex part. Perhaps that was why they were missing or incomplete. But why would she go to that trouble?

The following morning I was running a slight fever, and Andrés insisted on calling the doctor. It was just the flu, but for the next three days I had a very high temperature. One minute I would think I was better, but as soon as I got out of bed I was again attacked by bursts of fever and chills. One night I dreamed about two women in a procession, holding hands and wearing white tunics. The scene was somewhat ritualistic, you could hear the jingling of bracelets, and when they turned, although I could not see their faces, I knew they were both dead.

I finally started feeling better on the fourth day. I got up, took a shower, and dressed. And then I started to clean up the room. The mother-of-pearl jewelry box Adriana had refused to take was on the computer table. I did not know whether I wanted to keep it. I put it on the bed and opened it. I looked again at the old floor plans of the house and decided to keep them. I read some bland fragments of family postcards and threw them in the trash; I did the same with the rest of the papers. Finally, I shook the box to get rid of some pins and lint. A piece of paper was stuck to the bottom, stapled to one of the corners. I detached and opened it. It was a note written in black ink, in slanted and small handwriting:

My beloved,
Now we will forever be two hearts joined into one.

Underneath was an initial in a complicated stroke that vanished into the paper's worm-eaten edges. It could have been an *E*, but it also could have been an *F*.

There was no class the following Friday. Lidia came by the house to let me know poor Franca had suffered a stroke and was in the hospital. The prognosis was uncertain for now, her niece had told her. I was really sorry. I was sure I had discovered a crime, at least partially—I would never know with certainty the agreements and disagreements between them, nor how Brunner figured in the story—and I had a morbid desire to see the skeleton again.

I bombarded Andrés with my conclusions. He listened to me with more attention now, but like a good devil's advocate he objected to all my conjectures.

His principal objection was the same as mine: Why would Brunner's wife go to such trouble? If she had reduced him to bones, why didn't she just throw them in the garbage? And what about those little curls of black wire that seemed so revelatory to me? Simple repairs, Andrés would say. Like a hardworking wife who, instead of mending his socks, mended his skeleton.

"What about the hand we found here, how does that fit?" he would ask sarcastically.

"That? A sinister gift between accomplices. Or just a coincidence."

I did not give up, and in my spare time, surfing the Internet, I found a possible answer to the first objection. "For a forensic anthropologist, bones speak: all of life's events are stamped there, from before birth until after death."

Franca would not have wanted to run the risk of recognition (the more bones spread around, the more evidence beyond her control). Besides, maybe she took a secret pleasure in having Brunner exhibited there.

My leave from the magazine was about to end and I started getting some requests around that time, a series of notes on distance learning among others, so for a few days I was distracted from my own drama

One Saturday morning, I passed, by chance, in front of Giacomo's shop. When he saw me, he waved hello and gestured for me to approach. He wanted to introduce me to his partner Padeletti, who was on a stool drinking *mate*.

"This is Ms. Julia, Paddy, the one I told you about who lives in the house that was Clarisa's. She also knows Franca."

Paddy was about seventy and quite ravaged. He had a half-closed eye, and it took him a ton of effort to even get up and say hello. "Ah, a piece of work, those two women," he said.

"Giacomo told me you were friends—that you saw Brunner as a patient."

"He was a genius. You don't know what hands he had; you'd leave after each session feeling like new . . . I hope he's with his Chilean woman and not where I imagine!" he sighed.

I was in a hurry to go. However, I could not resist asking a crucial question: "Excuse my curiosity, but did you see the skeleton in his office?"

Paddy first looked at me with surprise, and then burst out laughing until a tear flowed from his half-closed eye. He dried the tear on his sleeve and looked at me with a mocking air. "You're referring to Jacinto, the quiet man?"

I was taken aback. Who was this Jacinto?

"That's what he called it," Paddy explained. "He'd say it was his best friend. The only one who didn't complain about bone pain. He was always joking with that poor skeleton."

And in a single instance, all my theories were shattered. I left feeling defeated and decided not to say a word about it to Andrés. After all, I had merely discovered the sad story of a secret love.

About six months after that meeting with Paddy, the magazine asked me to do a second part for the article on distance learning. Among other schools, I had to visit one at the border between Parque Chas and Agronomy that had joined the program. The principal's name was Mimi; she was an affable woman, and was delighted to have a journalist visit. We talked for half an hour about the project and the way her school would participate, and before leaving, she insisted on showing me the classrooms where they would record some of the lessons. Thanks to the donations of many others, she told me, they now had a good deal of educational material, especially in the areas of geography and the sciences. As soon as she opened the door to the natural sciences department, I saw it: a skeleton hanging on its hook.

I stood captivated in front of it. "Is it real?" I asked.

"No. There's likely only a few of those left; this one's quite old, but it must be made of resin or plastic. And it's almost complete. Other than that, it's a mystery."

I could barely breathe. "A mystery?"

"Yes, it showed up by itself." She laughed. "I mean, we never found out who brought it in. It appeared one morning at the school door, packed in a box. Like an abandoned baby."

EX OFFICIO

BY ARIEL MAGNUS
Balvanera

Translated by John Washington

He barely heard the scream, and he didn't hear the gunshot at all, or he didn't think it was a gunshot that he was hearing, which is what happens when you live in the midst of an unending stream of chaos that is the interior patio of an apartment building in Bajo Flores—there's no point in trying to make sense of all the racket, which makes this very public space, paradoxically, a perfect spot to commit a murder without anybody even noticing; hardly hearing the scream and then only retrospectively interpreting the previous noise as a gunshot, enabled him to conclude that the subsequent sound was that of a body hitting the ground. Lichi lifted himself off the couch and stuck his head out the single window in his studio apartment. The silence was so complete it startled him: for the first time since he and his father moved to this tiny apartment in Bajo Flores he couldn't hear a single radio playing, or even a dog barking; no plates were crashing against each other, and nobody was arguing on the telephone with their ex. Such extravagances of silence only occurred in moments immediately after a terrible tragedy.

It was three in the afternoon on a Sunday, as gray as every day in this building with its interior patio not much more spacious than an airshaft, which is what folks in this city called the holes of stink and shadow that were meant to ventilate the most overcrowded and foul buildings in the barrio. The typical thing to do would be to play the fool, or *roll into a ball*, as they say in these parts, which is the second most popular sport in the country, just after that other sport you also play with a ball, but Lichi didn't choose to be a cop to skirt the responsibility that was thrust at him, even when he wasn't in uniform, whether here or in China. So, dressed to stay in, he left his apartment and rang his neighbor's bell. If it was some hope of glory that pushed him out the door, the hope of single-handedly solving a crime and then possibly jumping up in rank was the fantasy of a real fool.

A short woman, almost as young as he was, answered the door with a baby in one hand and a revolver in the other. If he would have walked out in his underwear Lichi couldn't have felt more naked than he felt now, without his gun. What frightened him most was that the revolver was ancient, looking as if it belonged in a museum, one of those objects a person would inherit and not even know how to use.

"Sorry, I thought it was my ex-husband," the woman said, tucking the gun into a pocket. "Come on in."

In the six months that he'd been living in the building, Lichi, on his way to and from work, had only exchanged a casual hello with this woman, which led him to conclude that he inspired more confidence in her dressed as he was than in his police uniform, which is one of the least respected uniforms in the country, excepting, perhaps, the dust smock of a rural elementary schoolteacher.

He accepted the invitation to enter, not as part of his investigation, but because of plain and simple curiosity—in and out of this apartment strolled more children than would fit standing up, and he wanted to know how many actually lived there.

He counted seven, each a few inches taller than the last, like Russian dolls laid out on display, but all of them so quiet and still that they seemed like a single child, and certainly not an Argentinian one. His hunch turned out to be correct; they were from Peru, or so he concluded from the little flag stuck on top of the television playing a Peruvian music channel. What explained how so many kids could keep so quiet—which is what most surprised Lichi—was that the apartment, as small as it was, was chock-full of merchandise. Not even the craftiest little tyke could have scampered between those stacks. Bundles and bundles of all types of product were leaned against the walls, even blocking out the single window in the apartment. Depending on their size and durability, the bundles even served as the absent furniture: tables and chairs, shelves, couch, and even beds. The smell of packing tape was even stronger than the spice emanating from a pot meant to serve eight people.

"I was just looking for a toothpick," Lichi said, bumping into the bundle that was partially blocking the door and trying to figure out not if these products were legal, but to what level of illegality they belonged, and to thus decide if the thieves merited forgiveness, for stealing from other thieves, or another turn in jail.

"Could you help me lift this package?" the woman asked, pointing to an open space between the ceiling and a tower of floor rags.

Lichi wasn't bothered; it was, rather, a relief that the neighbor didn't wait too long to make it clear why she'd invited him in. Acting the gentleman, he leaned down, thrust his chest out like a weightlifter, and then, with a wink, asked for help from the largest of the little dwarves, who probably wasn't any older than eight. And then, after heaving the thing up, he wished the kid had lent a hand, as the package of what-nots was surprisingly and almost unmanageably heavy. He was a slim man, and lifting the bundle up and into the right nook was harder than dragging his drunk father to bed last night.

"Did you hear anything anomalous a moment ago?" Lichi asked, trying to catch his breath before leaving.

"I heard a scream," the woman admitted after a moment of thought, perhaps generated by Lichi's use of the word *anomalous*. "It probably came from the crazy lady on the second floor. It sounded like they were killing her. Which is why I thought it was my ex-husband—that he'd gotten the floors mixed up."

Lichi took leave by tipping a hat he wasn't wearing, and then climbed the stairs to the next floor. There were three apartments that faced (acoustically speaking) the crime scene, and he didn't know which to start with. Just as he was about to hit the switch again, a light flicked on: if the Peruvian woman said that her husband might have been confused about the apartment, it had to be the one directly above. He pressed the bell.

He immediately heard a groan, and then a shuffling. In the next apartment a dog started barking. He rang the bell again, instinctively peering in through the peephole, as if he would be able to see inside. Which is probably why he was not surprised that this was actually the case: they had installed the peephole backward (or maybe the door was installed backward). But he couldn't see much, just a hallway with, at the end of it, the legs of someone sitting in a wheelchair. The legs quickly disappeared and in their place a bald man with a thick beard came into view.

When the door finally opened, the light turned back off (the light timer was like an old man's bladder, Lichi thought, thinking of his father again, who was probably, if his drunkenness permitted, about ready to get up to take a leak). The only remaining light in the apartment was dim, and came from the opposite corner, which didn't give Lichi a clear view of the man's face as he explained to him that he'd heard a scream and was coming to make sure that nothing bad had occurred. It would have helped to be able to see the man's face, because he remained silent.

"May I?" Lichi asked, forgetting that he wasn't wearing his uniform, and that he didn't have a good reason (or a warrant) to search the place.

It took him a few more seconds to realize that the man didn't understand Spanish, and so he gave him his first lesson—less about the language than about the idiosyncrasies of the country—by walking in without further formalities. Compared with the last apartment, this one was almost empty, with just a few drapes hanging from the walls and a couple carpets under the sparse furniture, which looked as if it was made out of toothpicks. And yet the oppressive air was thick, almost unbearable. Lichi felt it in his stomach, his chest, even before he got up the nerve to peek his head into the kitchen and see the wheelchair, which was now squeezed between the freezer and a scratched Formica folding table. The skinny legs sitting in the chair were bare all the way up the thigh, provoking in Lichi a brief erotic fantasy (which he would never confess to, not even to himself), and belonged to a woman whose arms and face were disfigured by a horrible sickness, one of those sicknesses Lichi was glad he didn't even know the name of. She had her hair chopped seemingly at random, her gaze was fixed on the ceiling, she was drooling, and—her only sign of personality—a green hoop earring hung from a horribly swollen ear. What seemed at first to be a sash, wrapped around her green tunic at the level of her flat chest, turned out to be a belt tying her to the chair. And there was no doubt that the cloth wrapped around her mouth was a homemade gag.

"She wanted to," said a veil-covered woman who appeared around the corner and must have been the mother.

Moved by the fact that inherited looks, from parent to child, would survive such a deforming sickness (it's all about the genes), Lichi hesitated a few seconds before grasping that the woman did speak Spanish, unlike her husband, and was giving Lichi an explanation before he even asked for one. He was tempted to ask her what the poor girl had wanted, if she wanted them to tie her up, gag her, or both, but the question provoked a bit of dark pleasure in him, and he kept quiet.

"She wanted to . . ." the woman repeated like a mantra. Then she repeated herself yet again.

As she proceeded to slowly untie the cloth around her daughter's mouth, and as if she were wondering whether or not the daughter would understand that she needed to behave herself in front of a visitor, the father offered Lichi a tiny cup of tea that he seemed to have pulled out of his pocket, just as certain waiters can hand out a plate of gnocchi or steak and fries almost as soon as you order them. They seemed to feel such guilt about the state of their daughter that Lichi started to feel guilty himself, though mostly about his presence in their space. He would have gotten out of there if the offering of tea hadn't tied him even more tightly, though subtly, than the belt around the twisted limbs of the young woman.

"You didn't notice, a few moments ago, the sound of a gunshot?" Lichi took the opportunity to ask the potential witnesses.

"The crazy lady below us is the one with the gun," the mother said, with about the same disdain the neighbor had used to talk about her daughter.

Suddenly another shot rang out, much louder than before, and Lichi deduced that it must have come from a higher floor (though sound, he knew, rises). He hurried to finish his tea (leaving tea in a cup so tiny, he imagined, could be taken for an unpardonable offense in these people's culture) and said goodbye to the family. Sure that he would run across other neighbors, all of whom would be asking what had just happened, or maybe even already standing over a cadaver, intensified the state of emptiness in which he found the hallway. Standing in front of the stairway he felt himself facing another dilemma: maybe he should forget the whole thing and go back to his apartment, at least to make sure that his dad could make it to the bathroom and not wet the bed.

It was his legs that sent the command to his head to climb the next flight of stairs and figure out, no matter the consequences, what the cause of these shots was, even if it meant putting himself at risk. Who else these days, not limiting ourselves to police officers (and not counting rural schoolteachers) actually worked *ex officio*, as they say, and put themselves at risk? The closest example Lichi could think of to actually doing what should be done, without anybody demanding it of you or threatening you, was the slogan and strategy *Work by rule*, used by the union of drivers (by which they exaggeratedly followed *all* the rules, down to the most minute regulation) as a protest when they wanted a salary increase. Completing basic obligations in this country had, paradoxically, become a way to go on strike.

On the third floor, the hall light certainly wasn't working by the rules. The only light at all was leaking out through the peepholes. Everything seemed to be dark, even, Lichi noticed, inside the door that was partially open in front of him. He leaned in and pushed it slightly, and then when he glanced down he saw a trace of blood on the floor. Following the blood back into the hallway he saw that the trail turned from a line into sparse drops down the hallway, which must have been the direction the shot person took after trying to staunch their wound.

The path went right back to the staircase, not from the stairs Lichi had just walked up, but the stairs continuing to the next floor. It was terra incognita for Lichi, who had never gone up past the second floor, but who tended to take the stairs instead of the elevator. He ascended them, surprised once again at not meeting another soul, making it all the way to the roof, where recently hung laundry was swaying from a line. Following the same impulse that made him bound up the three flights, he searched every inch of the roof, which wasn't much to speak of—the combined space of all six apartments on a floor, plus the hallway, equaled about the size of a single apartment in a better neighborhood, which would be almost any other neighborhood in the entire city.

He leaned against the railing to rest, pulled out a cigarette, looked in vain for a lighter, put the cigarette to his lips, and inhaled, imagining the smoke hitting his lungs. But it was mere imagination, as was looking for the owner of the clothes—as if hanging them to dry on the roof were a crime. (Which it was, in the strict sense, or at least members of the building's committee had discussed the possibility of closing the roof off after it had been revealed that women had been walking on it in heels, which was puncturing the membrane, though, in this case, he couldn't really justify working *ex officio*.) And he couldn't justify anything by the trail of blood either, as, in the daylight, he could now see that it was just drops of dirty water—probably darkened by some badly dyed piece of clothing.

As if actually smoking his cigarette, Lichi paused another

moment to look down at the street, so much more desolate and gray compared to the colorful chaos of traffic, markets, vendors, and strollers that brought the city to life during the week. The workday bustle was so vibrant that it reverberated in the graffiti of the rolltop security doors, in the nameplates of the businesses screaming on the walls, and in the dirty and broken sidewalks. The streets weren't simply empty, but were rather full of emptiness—tumultuous solitude—like a theater hours before or after a show. The street was an unlit cigarette! Or a knockoff electronic cigarette, exactly what was sold on these streets.

In that thick silence, Lichi was a bird's-eye witness to an armed robbery. A girl walking down the street was surprised by two delinquents who appeared out of thin air (for all the similarities in this country between the police and thieves, in this, Lichi thought, they are exact opposites—the law announces itself from far away by its lights and sirens, chasing away any danger, thus never catching it). As one of the young delinquents pointed a fake-looking .22 at the girl—even from this distance it looked like one of the toy guns they sold in the shops on this very street—the other snagged her handbag, flipped through it with the alacrity of a customs agent who doesn't like his job, and found what he was looking for. Fifteen seconds later the two had already evaporated and the girl, her mouth open to let loose a scream that never came, tripped over a crack in the sidewalk and almost fell into the street. But not even that perilous tumble awoke in Lichi the impulse to go to her aid, perhaps because it all happened in complete silence, as if a scene from a silent movie. He saw the woman walk away as if nothing had happened, and then Lichi flicked the cigarette off the side of the roof as if he'd actually smoked it.

He went back down the stairs, feeling with each step more and more surprise by his passivity about a crime committed before his very eyes, especially when he was looking for a more illusory crime, a crime he knew only by sound. The materiality of what he had just seen influenced his interpretation of the third shot that he heard that Sunday, just as he was rounding the bend of the staircase on the fifth floor. He rang the bell of the apartment the sound had come from, knowing now that the noise wasn't from a gun, but from someone who was trying to imitate the noise of a gun. The door opened right away, as if somebody had been expecting him.

"Are you coming about the gunshots?" an enthused young man wearing an oversized Colombian national jersey asked. "You don't know how happy you're making me. I'm doing a series of YouTube tutorials on how to make homemade sounds, I mean completely homemade, with nothing but things lying around your place. I've made rain, thunder, shoe squeaks, a spaceship, but I couldn't figure out how to do a gunshot. Because, you know, popping a balloon or smacking a belt against the table doesn't work. Not even a Zippo or a stapler sounds much like the cocking of a gun. And who even actually keeps balloons in their house, right? After looking hard, though, I finally found a good recipe. But I wasn't going to be satisfied until a neighbor got scared and came to see who I was killing."

Lichi, ears ringing with the Caribbean chatter (for him, the Caribbean started anywhere north of Rio), put on his best fool face (his usual face, as many would say) took out a pack of cigarettes, and told the kid that he didn't come about any noises, but was just looking for a light.

"I didn't realize until I got up to the roof that I didn't bring my lighter," he said, enjoying his small triumph that someone else would feel more like a fool than he did.

Surprised, but not doubting for a moment that he was hearing the truth, the YouTuber stuck his hand into his pocket and pulled out a Zippo. As he flicked the lighter a few times before getting a flame, both men noticed that the noise was nearly identical to the cocking of a gun. Weren't these, Lichi thought to himself, the lighters American soldiers used in Vietnam? With the pretext of making a lighter that would stay lit even on windy days, they had designed them to make prisoners of war extra nervous during torture sessions. He thought of mentioning this piece of trivia to the kid, but opted for something more relevant.

"The best way to reproduce the noise of a pistol is to make noise with a pistol, and in this part of town, everyone already has one in his home," he shared, as a way of thanking the kid, and as a way of imparting a lesson in Argentinian civility—in the end, he figured, everybody finds the teacher he or she deserves.

Instead of going back up, he went down the steps deliberately, slowly, doing his best to enjoy the tobacco before returning to his apartment, where his dad wouldn't let him smoke. He wouldn't let him do anything, really, except of course fulfilling his filial duties and taking care of him, which he seemed, intentionally, to make difficult. Which is why Lichi—tired of searching for and tossing out the bottles of sake his dad snuck into the house—let him get drunk again last night.

The slow descent let Lichi think again about, and even solve, the case of the light-shaft mystery. When he passed by the floor with the young woman in the wheelchair, he understood that what she had wanted was the earring hanging from her ear, which had left it as swollen as a tomato. Lichi preferred not to even imagine what they had used to do the piercing, but it was clear to him now that whatever it was had provoked the scream that he heard, and then the scream had provoked the gag. When he passed by the apartment of the Peruvians he realized that the package he had restored was surely what had fallen after the scream, and after the gunshot. Which is how the crime must have occurred, and the crime scene, he realized, was none other than the interior patio of his own brain. He was the perpetrator and the detective, and, come to think of it, even the victim.

In front of his own apartment's door he stopped for a moment to look into his peephole, not so much to check if it was inverted, and it was, but to finish his cigarette. What he saw was terrifying: his father had fallen out of bed and seemingly knocked his head against the iron chair that served as his nightstand. He was bleeding abundantly, staining the carpet red. Given the position of his arm, it could be deduced that his last effort was in reaching for his son's phone, though who knows who he'd been planning to call.

Lichi, preparing to drop his cigarette and snub it out, decided instead to light himself another and continue walking toward the street. He suddenly remembered that he needed to buy a few things, and figured that the Chinese mart on the corner was probably open (his countrymen were the only ones who worked hard in Argentina). But then he thought that he'd better go into the office and file a report about the crime he'd witnessed from the roof. And he could even tell them about the crime he solved in his apartment building—surely his colleagues would get a kick out of it, and tell him he'd acted the fool (they were already calling him Lichi, as if he were a fruit, so how much worse could it get?). What mattered was delaying, for as long as possible, returning to his apartment, so that everybody would know that the only reason he had been absent for so long was because he was fulfilling his duty.

FURY OF THE WORM

BY ALEJANDRO PARISI

Mataderos

Translated by John Washington

T he merry-go-round spun with the same laziness that seemed to seep out of the miserable tin-and-brick shacks, the dying grass, the scattered trash, and out of all the people and dogs living in the barrio. The ride spun and spun, slave to its brief orbit, its constant twist: the horsies rising and dipping, squeaking sharply; a paint-chipped sleigh reflecting the sun from its metallic incrustations; and a little airplane, unmoving, without propeller, trembling as the children jumped into it. From its depths, the same song sang out loudly, with an almost exaggerated stridence.

Leaning his shoulder against a post, Ángel Camaño watched the young mothers who stood at the side of the ride, helping, smacking, caressing, or nudging their children along. It was hot. Ángel Camaño wiped his forehead with a swatch of orange cloth. His clear eyes, an almost translucent turquoise, gazed at the brown, smiling faces of the children, who were reaching up and lunging at the ring he swung down at them. Camaño smiled, proud of himself for his work, for his dedication.

For years he had been a schoolteacher, until he had to leave the Mission. After living for a decade as a nomad, he settled in Los Perales and bought the merry-go-round, even taking on the debts the previous owner couldn't pay. Now he was the darling and master of the ride.

Slowly, the ride stopped spinning. When it made its last turn, Ángel Camaño offered candy to the kids, who gobbled them up and let him pinch their cheeks. Looking happily at the cluster of smiles, Camaño announced that the next ride would be free for everyone. There was an explosion of screams and laughter. The young mothers, however, were already gathering up their kids and starting to walk away.

Confused, Camaño hung the ring on the hook nailed into the black and green–painted post—the same color theme of the entire merry-go-round—and stepped out of the shady refuge of the ride. That was when he saw, curiously, the motorcycles zooming toward him across the barren landscape. When the four bikes skidded to a stop just outside the ring of the merry-go-round, Camaño opened his arms into the shape of a cross to give the men a warm welcome.

"Hello, fellas," he said with a smile.

One of the young men got off his bike, looked both ways, and then stepped forward. Obese, dressed in basketball shorts and a jersey, the man known as Shrek pointed a short-muzzled revolver at Camaño. "You're screwed, Ángelito," he said.

Camaño looked at his watch. Four fifteen in the afternoon. Not a bad time to die: all across the country little kids were playing in the sun. He glanced around, but all he could see was the flat gray of the shuttered hospital, about two hundred yards away. His destiny, like that of everybody else in the neighborhood, had set on its course in that building.

The other three men got off their bikes and took out their guns. They all aimed at Camaño. With his eyes closed, he awaited the gunshots. But nobody pulled the trigger. The young men surrounded him. Shrek tied his hands with a cable that one of the others hooked to the back of a motorcycle.

That was when Ángel Camaño felt the fear, more fear than all the fear he had ever felt in his life.

The bikes started up. He tried to follow behind, but he couldn't keep up. He caught sight of the merry-go-round, now far behind him. The rocks and ground tore at his back and body as the men dragged him to Worm's hideout, high, high, high up in Los Perales.

Inhaling the smoke deep into his lungs, leaning his elbows out the window, which was without a frame or glass, Worm peered out at the immensity before him. Ever since he could remember, this view was the most beautiful he could imagine. Years ago, when he was just an orphan living in a shack with his grandpa, he would sneak into that huge ramshackle building—originally meant to be one of the best hospitals in Latin America, but which had started falling apart as soon as it was built—scamper up the first floor past the doctors, and climb all the way up ten flights. They hadn't ever really finished with the initial construction, which would make him, even today, have to duck loose sprigs of steel that had oxidized after half a century of abandonment, before he reached the window and was able to look out onto the city. It was simultaneously so close and so far from him, so far from Luchito, as he used to be known— the young man who had once been so small and so lost.

But that was years ago, and now he didn't look at the city in fear. On the contrary: he knew that the houses, the neighborhood, and everything he could see from that window was his. He didn't get it easily. If there was something Luchito learned as he converted into Worm, it was that you paid the price of rising to power in blood, and he had seen many of his boys bleed themselves out on those streets below him. Now he had an army of fifty. They called themselves the Renegade

Boys. Thieves, dealers, killers, chieftains, soccer hooligans, government pawns . . . sometimes he could even surprise himself with all the different work they did.

Worm slowly exhaled the smoke from his lungs, and then let out a cough.

Scattered across the room behind him, a handful of Renegades killed time on their phones, smoking, snorting, or sitting in front of a soccer game being played on the sixty-four inch screen on the wall. From another room came the methodical noise of the three Renegades tasked with prepping and packing kilo bags of coke they needed to deliver to a downtown barrio that night. Worm looked at all his men, feeling pride at the heights he had achieved—so tall, so high, towering over all of Los Perales.

In one corner, Marco Antonio Cuellar was wringing his hands, unable to hide his fear. Maybe it was the fact that he was surrounded by so many Argentinians. That neighborhood was a Russian doll, full of all sorts of distinct people who hardly ever mixed. Which is why Worm was so surprised to receive Cuellar's request. The Bolivians worked and lived on the margins, going in and out of the central market, loaded up with vegetables, trailed by their children, or cooped up in hidden workshops where they sewed clothes they would sell downtown. Worm had taken note of their work ethic, their unfaltering obedience, as if toiling all day could slip them out of the poverty that had been dragging them down for centuries.

Which is why, with Cuellar's request, Worm saw an opportunity. After all, he wouldn't deny a favor to anybody. Especially to somebody who ruled the area of the neighborhood that the Renegades didn't have control over, but were looking to gain access to. Worm had learned that things always got complicated, which is why it was always good to have a loaded gun and a safe place to hide.

He took another drag off his joint and approached Cuellar. "You want a hit?"

"No thanks," the Bolivian said, eyes locked on the butt of the gun Worm had tucked into the waistband of his Nueva Chicago shorts.

"Relax, Bolivia."

"Did you already take care of it?"

"Don't be nervous. You'll see." Worm put a hand on Cuellar's back.

"But you told me—"

Worm raised a hand up and Cuellar, startled, stopped midsentence. "You came," Worm said, "because the cops wouldn't do shit for you. That's where the Bolivians and the Argentinians come together. And now you want justice, so you're going to have to trust in the Worm."

He coughed again, cleared his throat, inhaled, and went to the window to spit. He could see the bikes on their way. He took another hit, coughed, and then turned around and said, "Here they are."

They pulled Camaño in still tied up, covered in blood and bruises. Shrek attached the cable that bound Camaño's hands together to a column. Ángel Camaño tried to stand up, but one of the Renegades kicked him in the knee, and he fell back to the ground.

Everybody was silent, wondering why Worm had gone to so much effort when they could have killed the guy with a simple shot to the head.

"Worm," Camaño muttered, "I work for you."

"Quiet," Worm responded. He turned away to look for Cuellar, who wasn't in sight. "*Mamani*, Bolivia, come here, damnit!"

Behind the Renegades, Cuellar was paralyzed, his eyes fixed on the floor.

"Is that him?" Worm asked, motioning to Camaño.

Cuellar looked up. "Yes sir," he said, without moving.

Furious, Worm walked up to Cuellar, grabbed him by a shoulder, and pulled him over to Camaño, who was drooling blood and snot. Worm pulled him upright.

"You look like a four of cups, Ángelito," Worm said to Camaño. And then, turning to Cuellar: "He's yours."

Cuellar's Bolivian features blanched. "But sir, we had agreed . . ."

"How old is your little girl?" Worm asked. "Six? Seven?"

Cuellar shook his head, unable to handle it all.

"Look at him, damnit!" Worm shouted. Even the Renegades were fearful.

Finally, Cuellar glanced up at Ángel Camaño, who was trying to say something, but was silenced by Worm, who knocked him with the butt of his pistol and said: "Look at his legs, his hands. Those are the hands that took the life of your little girl." He turned to a Renegade and barked: "Pull his pants down!"

Two of the Renegades jumped up and started undressing Camaño. His skin was shredded, torn up by rocks and debris. He was caked in blood and smelled sharply of fear. Camaño cried out, asking Worm to take pity. "Please . . ."

The Renegades formed a semicircle around the three men.

Worm spoke up again: "Look at him, man. Look at him good. There's the dick that went in your little girl. Who's going to take care of this now? You or me?"

Cuellar couldn't hold back his tears. Worm smiled. He could see that Cuellar's rage had turned to shame, to hopelessness.

"You want to kill him, don't you?"

Cuellar nodded.

"Good. Good." Worm placed a hand on his back. "But you know what? Your daughter suffered, and now she'll never be able to forget this son of a bitch. If you kill him, it's over in a moment. Which is why we're going to do something else. Fideo . . ."

One of the Renegades, a tall, thin kid wearing an Argentina soccer jersey, left the huddle of men for the other room, returning a moment later with a broom.

"Grab it, man," Worm said to Cuellar, who looked on, terrified. "Some things you got to do on your own. You have to be the one to avenge your daughter, *Mamani*. Come on, boys, hold him tight 'cause he's gonna shake like a dog."

Shrek and two other men approached Camaño, who was twisting, trying to break loose, calling out, "Worm, let me go and I'll work for you for free until I die!"

Worm didn't respond. Turning to Cuellar, he said, "Now, *Mamani*. You're going to let him feel what your daughter felt. Grab the broom and stick it so far up his ass it comes out his mouth."

Cuellar started to cry. To cry and look around, searching for a way out. Worm approached carefully and whispered something in his ear that nobody else could hear. The Bolivian walked up to Camaño, took the broomstick, and whacked him, hard, in the back, whacked him one, two, three times.

"That's it, that's it . . ." Worm said encouragingly.

Already exhausted, Cuellar dropped the broom. He felt like he was going to faint—he wanted to end it.

Worm snuck back up to him. He crouched down, grabbed the broom, and handed it back to Cuellar, ordering, "Now do what I told you."

"That's enough. You can take it from here."

"Do it!" Worm yelled. "Your daughter deserves revenge. You told me yourself when you came to see me. Do it, you piece of shit."

Camaño struggled, cried, but the Renegades had him pressed against the floor, his legs and arms open wide. Suddenly, all the Renegades in the room started to chant, "*Shove it up his ass, shove it up his ass . . .*"

Cuellar looked around in fear and disgust.

"Think about your girl," Worm said. "Give it to him. Shove it in. Make it come out his mouth." Even some of the other Renegades seemed surprised by Worm's intensity.

Finally, lost in some other place, crying and asking for forgiveness from God and the Virgin Mary, Marco Antonio Cuellar shoved the broom handle into Camaño's ass, pulling it out and then shoving it back in, harder and harder.

Camaño's screams blended with the whistles and applause of the Renegades, who started to spit and kick at him with their brand-new tennis shoes. This lasted nearly twenty minutes, until Cuellar fell to the floor, unable to contain himself, his fear, his sadness, his shame, his pain. Camaño was unconscious, maybe dead, laid out in a pool of blood and fecal matter.

Worm came up and helped Cuellar to his feet.

"Give him a glass of wine," he demanded, and one of the Renegades immediately handed the Bolivian a glass.

Cuellar drank it in one gulp, and then continued to cry. "Why?" he asked, his voice broken.

"Because the world has gone to shit, and we need to clean it up every once in a while. Now you're going to walk away like a man. You did what you had to do. And that lump of shit will remember this for the rest of his life."

"You're not going to kill him?"

"Maybe he's already dead. If he wakes up, he's going to go back to work for me. What he's *not* going to do is touch anybody in your family ever again."

"But . . . I didn't even want to . . ." Cuellar whimpered.

Worm put a hand on his shoulder and said softly, "Your little girl didn't want to either. But you know what happened. And now that's taken care of. Get back to your life, *Mamani*. When I need you, I'll come looking. Understood?"

Unable to speak, Cuellar nodded. And then, suddenly, he vomited, and scurried away, not wanting to see any more of what he had done.

Little by little, the Renegades returned to their Playstation, to their cell phones, to cutting and packing baggies.

Camaño's stink started making Worm feel nauseous. He lit another joint and took a hit. He had seen, done, and ordered much worse things than Camaño had just suffered, but he felt sad for some reason, or something like sad, and he didn't want to give in to the feeling.

He went back to the window to get some fresh air. The day had started to darken outside. The violet sky spread over all of Los Perales, over Mataderos, over the entire capital.

He peered down. In the dirt wasteland below him a group of kids were playing soccer. Watching them, Worm remembered playing in that same open field.

"We need to do something with this," Shrek said.

Worm didn't respond.

"Take him to the hospital or something," Shrek said. "Camaño is still useful to us. We should do something." Seeing that Worm wasn't responding, he added, "Everything okay?"

Nothing. Worm was too far away. He smiled as far below him one of the kids swerved through the defense and scored a goal. The boy celebrated by holding his hands behind his ears, as if trying to better hear the roaring of the crowd, a crowd that, Worm knew well, would never give him anything.

Worm leaned halfway out the window and screamed down, "Sweet goal, kid!"

The players, excited that Worm was watching their game, whistled up to him from below.

"Help . . ." Worm heard a thin voice call from behind.

Seeing Camaño on his knees, Worm thought about how the world would always be this shithole, starting with the worst areas of the neighborhood, and then, sooner or later, swallowing up even those cheerful kids playing soccer down below, just as it had swallowed him.

"What do you want us to do, Worm?" Shrek asked.

Only then did Worm take out his gun and fire three, four, five shots, spilling Camaño's guts onto the floor of the building, shooting up there so high, so high up in Los Perales.

PART II

CRIMES? OR MISDEMEANORS?

A FACE IN THE CROWD

BY PABLO DE SANTIS

Caballito

Translated by John Washington

E ver since he was young, Nigro liked protests and rallies—
snapping photos through the acid fog of tear gas or under
the rainfall of police clubs and rocks. Once, a rubber
bullet hit him in his left thigh, and he had to go to the hospital. When he reached his fifties, however, work turned calm
and monotonous: he mostly shot interviews, people on love
seats sipping coffee.

He also did a weekly photo shoot on Saturdays called "A
Face in the Crowd." He captured images of places thronging
with people: Florida Street at noon, the interior of subway
cars at seven thirty in the morning, the Lavalle theaters on
Saturday nights, the people who got off the 11 train every
morning at dawn. While other photographers captured empty
beaches or inanimate objects, he preferred photos where there
wasn't space to move. He liked tightness, breathlessness. He
searched for the moment when one person (just a single face
in the whole crowd) looked up at the camera. Everybody else
was oblivious that he was shooting them, except for that one
person who discovered his lens and looked on with curiosity,
with indifference, or even with alarm.

The first envelope came to the office along with the regular
mail. His name, *Norberto L. Nigro,* was written by hand in a

neat, black cursive. There was no return address. Inside the envelope was a 5x7 photo. At first he thought that an "artist" must have sent it to him. He and Orsini, his boss, would laugh at "artistic" photographers who substituted reality for artifice, the figurative for the abstract, who intruded on the silence of photographs with long, abstruse explanations. These artists shot the foot of a chair, a traffic light turning green, clothes hung out on a balcony, and then they put together shows and called them things like "Manifestation of the Visible," "The Borders of the Real," or "The Darkness of Light."

But the photo in the envelope didn't have a title or a signature. It was just a simple shot of water in a swimming pool.

The second photograph, as anonymous as the first, came a week later. This time you could make out the edge of the pool. There was something odd in the angle of the take, as if the photographer had been pushed off balance. The photo had also been taken from a high point of view. With the first envelope, the lack of a return address could have been a mistake, but now Nigro knew it had been intentionally left off.

A few days later Orsini came across Nigro examining the third photograph—the roof of a merry-go-round with white-and-red horses weathered by rust and grime—and asked him what he was looking at. Nigro rummaged around in his desk drawer and showed him the other two photos, asking if anybody else in the office had received anything like them.

Orsini shook his head. "It's probably just some lunatic," he said.

"Lunatics usually say too much. This guy isn't saying anything," Nigro responded.

"Do you recognize the place?"

"It looks like some country club pool. I haven't been in a pool for thirty years."

"It must be a pool with a diving board. All these photos are from a high vantage point."

Orsini, never able to focus on anything for very long, forgot about the photos as soon as his phone rang.

They kept coming, one more in September, two in October, all as unpopulated as the first. Although there was nothing scary in the photos, and there wasn't any sign of a threat, Nigro felt a prickle of anxiety every time he opened a new envelope. They were like a series of letters in a secret message. He knew that an essential element of this message was that the photos were empty; there was not a single person in any of them.

It was the coffee vendor—a twenty-five-year-old idiot who specialized in interrupting conversations and spilling scalding coffee on your desk—who made the connection. Without anybody asking his opinion, he pointed to the photos that Nigro had laid out on his desk and said, "Maestro, now that you're taking shots of a pool, you should snap a couple with some girls in bikinis."

"They're not mine. I don't even know where they were taken."

"They're from Chacabuco Park."

"Are you sure?"

The coffee seller rearranged the photos on the desk as if aligning fragments of a map.

"The pool, the trees, the deck lounge, the roof of the merry-go-round—just a few steps away."

"Is there a diving board?"

"Three of them. One pretty high. The others lower."

Nigro went to the paper's archives to look for any news related to the pool in Chacabuco Park, something that could explain the ghostly photographs. The archivist delivered him a manila envelope full of articles on the construction of the highway that cut through the park, the damage it caused; the disappearance, back in the seventies, of a statue of a panther; the happy memories of a peanut vendor who had worked in the park for forty years. Once, a man was stabbed in a corner of the park, but it had happened two years before, and it was far from the pool. There were also a few photos of the pool and its diving boards.

The next Saturday, he walked from his neighborhood of Boedo to the park. The flowers of jacaranda and tipa trees had confettied the November sidewalks purple and yellow. When he arrived at the gate to the swimming pool, a worker with a gray apron told him that he couldn't go in, that the pool didn't open until the first Tuesday of December.

Nigro told the man that he just needed to snap one photo from the diving board to announce the beginning of the swimming season in the paper. He dropped a few made-up names of municipal authorities, and, succumbing to the onslaught of directors and subdirectors, the man in the gray apron let him in. He walked through the men's changing room that stank of chlorine, and opened the door that led to the pool. The diving board stood silently on the opposite side, as if waiting for him. When he finally made it to the exact point from which his anonymous correspondent had been taking the photographs, he would find, he knew, the answer to the riddle.

He climbed the steps uneasily—he was terrified of heights—and stepped onto the platform. Vertigo made his hands tremble. He took a quick picture of the bottom of the pool—without water, but with a few splashes of paint. He snapped a leafless tree, the weathered roof of the merry-go-round. Patiently, he replicated each of the photographs of his anonymous predecessor.

When he had taken them all he realized that he wasn't alone. There was a stranger, wearing a gray sweater despite the November heat, standing right behind him on the diving board. He looked a little over forty, and wore old-fashioned, square-framed glasses. He seemed serious, like he was concentrating on something, or trying to figure out what to say.

"I knew you'd finally make it," he finally said.

For a moment Nigro considered screaming, but it would have been too embarrassing. "Do we know each other?" he asked.

"No. This is the first time we're seeing each other. I'm from Misiones—a photographer, like yourself. But my photos don't make it into the paper. I work weddings, birthdays."

"Are you going to let me go down?"

"You came here to find out why I sent you those photos, and now all you want is to leave?"

"I'm scared of heights."

"That's something else we have in common."

Nigro stared at the guy. He was smaller than Nigro, but the platform was narrow enough that a shove would send both of them over the edge. *I should have waited until December,* he thought, *when the pool would have been filled with water.*

"Given your fear of heights," the man said, "I'll be quick. Three years ago at a wedding, I ran into an old friend from my teenage years. She was the bride. Seeing her again, I realized how much of my life I'd wasted. With some ridiculous excuse I took her out onto a patio to snap some photos, just the two of us, while the groom got drunk with his friends down below. After she came back from the honeymoon we saw each other again. Two years later we decided to run off together. We left a series of clues that would make people think we were living together in Italy. But we were actually just in a different part of Buenos Aires."

The man shrugged, peering down as if calculating the distance to the bottom of the pool.

"The husband would have kept on thinking we were in Europe, far away and out of reach. But one evening you took a shot of a car in the metro filled with tired people on their way home from work. She was the only one in the car who was looking at the camera. Do you remember that shot?"

"Buenos Aires is a big city."

"She had a sister who lived here, close to Congreso. After he found out she was still in town, her ex kept an eye on the sister's house until she showed up. It was in February. We had planned to meet at this pool, as we did twice a week. When she didn't show, I climbed up to the diving board to get a better view. She never came. Her husband confronted her as she walked out of her sister's house, called out her name, and when she turned he shot her in the forehead. Then he killed himself. You work for a newspaper, maybe you even covered the incident."

"Crime isn't my beat."

"You never put it together, did you? Even when looking at all my photographs together—that it was about waiting?" The man rubbed his hands together—the first sign that he was anxious. "You never realized that the place was always empty because I was waiting for a woman who would never show up?"

Nigro didn't respond: he didn't want to tell this guy that none of that had ever crossed his mind. The only reading he had ever come to with the photos had led to the ignorant steps he'd taken up the ladder and onto this diving board.

The man flinched; Nigro prepared to defend himself. His camera was heavy. If he swung it at the man's head . . . But any rapid movement would probably knock them both off the platform. The man's flinch, however, was just a nervous stepping out of the way, giving room for Nigro to pass. Nigro walked by him and started his slow descent down the concrete steps.

"Careful, Mr. Photographer. Those steps are only made for climbing up."

Nigro's feet started shaking and he hurried down. He wanted to get away, to erase this man from his mind.

When he was on level ground, he saw that the guy was still waiting up top, as if on guard.

A few days later Nigro received another envelope, which he opened very carefully. Inside was a clipping with one of his own photographs: a wooden car of the A line, six in the evening. Everybody in the photo was oblivious, except one woman staring at the camera, her eyes wide in fear.

A face in the crowd.

ORANGE IS A PRETTY COLOR

BY VERÓNICA ABDALA

Chacarita

Translated by John Washington

S he'd read it somewhere. And it was true: a person can handle whatever life deals them. She herself, Marina, could become a cold and vengeful woman, even while appearing quite the opposite. Like that time when her brother Germán lied to her about the death of her rabbit. He'd told her that it had fallen into the pool. Later, Marina learned that it wasn't true. A neighbor had seen her brother and his friend throw it in, but the neighbor hadn't been able to save the animal because she didn't know how to swim.

A few days after burying the rabbit, Marina hid a dead pigeon in Germán's backpack. She'd found it in the yard, picked it up using a plastic bag as a glove, and then slipped it into his backpack. Germán found it the next morning, before going to school. Marina had never seen him scream or sob with as much fear. She didn't care. She heard his first scream from the kitchen and then ran and locked herself in the bathroom. From inside she could hear her mother consoling her brother, and her father say that he'd take care of the bird. She smiled, maybe because she was nervous. The fracas only lasted a few minutes, and then they were hurried off to school, Germán with his eyes swollen from tears and, next to him, in the backseat, unmoved, Marina.

On that Saturday in May, she didn't think of that childhood memory until the moment she'd locked herself in the bathroom to do her nails and put on her makeup, while Guillermo was shuddering on the floor of the living room. She heard him crying, but unlike her brother, Guillermo hadn't screamed first.

That Saturday she had woken up at around nine. On weekends she usually liked to sleep in. Workdays, she had to wake up at seven and walk up Forest Avenue all the way to the sweater shop. On Forest there were rows of shops that sold, all year round, nothing but sweaters, sweatshirts, and jackets. She was in charge of retail at a store called Nevado. She made minimum wage, but didn't complain. It was enough to live a simple life with Guillermo, and even to splurge once in a while: a good dinner, a pretty dress, a weekend at Mar del Plata. They'd been together for eight years and she felt good with him, though at times she would think that the only men she could truly share her life with were Ramón, her hairdresser, and Roberto the doorman, who took care of the apartments and dealt with all the tenants in the Olleros building. Guillermo had become more and more apathetic over the years, sometimes seeming totally disinterested in her life or anything she told him. She was always the one to start conversations: about a news clip on TV, some neighborhood gossip, or a magazine article she'd read. Recently, everything she shared with him seemed to bore him. It's a mystery as to why, at a certain point in a relationship, a couple loses enthusiasm for each other, the magic a lost and distant memory. Guillermo, these days, seemed like he wasn't even there, but she kept on taking care of him, even more than before, especially once his health had started to deteriorate.

After the heart attack he suffered—two years ago, when he was forty-four—Marina made sure to buy vegetables and fresh fruit in the market next to the train station, and she made sure that their home was in shipshape condition, so that by the time he came home from work (he was a bank teller) he'd find the cat brushed and fed, everything clean, and food on the table—the menu always fat-free and low sodium.

He didn't seem to value what she did for him, or perhaps he just didn't even realize it, but she kept up her work. She didn't want anything at all to disturb him, though the most dangerous factor with his health was his smoking. He didn't take the suggestion to quit easily: he said that he couldn't give up his cigarettes like he couldn't give up who he was. He re-mained the same impulsive and irascible man as always, the jokester at work, the guy who could always make the ladies laugh.

Marina never would have imagined that that Saturday would be different than any other Saturday. The only thing out of the ordinary was that Gulliermo had gone to Tornú to get an electrocardiogram after feeling palpitations and shortness of breath in the middle of the night. She had been expecting a typical weekend, but then the fit of coughing came—at three in the morning. She bolted upright when she heard him start hacking. He was sitting on the edge of the bed with his hands on his chest and his eyes wide open, forcing the air to enter and exit his lungs, like he was trying to inflate an old burlap sack. She brought him a glass of water, and a few minutes later his color came back.

"I already feel a little better, but in the morning I should go to the hospital, calm myself down," he had said.

She agreed that it was a good idea to get it checked out. Surely the doctors would say that everything was fine and they could go out to eat as planned. She wanted to think the weekend would turn out like this. If it were up to him, they would just stay in, watching episode after episode of whatever television series they were into. Usually, though, she would insist that they go out for a walk, or grab brunch, and Guillermo would, like always, finally give in.

That Saturday morning, after Guillermo left, Marina stayed in bed, tossing and turning. The morning was chilly. She pulled the sheets and comforter over her head, stretched her legs out to one side and her torso to the other, feeling her spine stretch, and then she took a deep breath. She would spend the day relaxing, coddling Guillermo; it seemed like a good plan to her.

When she got up she went straight to the kitchen. The apartment was still. She opened the package of ground coffee, poured it into the coffee maker, and then stood there, hands planted on the counter as the vapor started to rise out of the machine. She poured herself a tall cup, added a splash of cold milk, and walked over to the kitchen table.

It was a small apartment: two bedrooms, a living room/kitchen decorated with two wooden bookshelves, a round table with three chairs, and a small sofa of brown chenille that Marina had decorated with some colorful pillows. On the table was the newspaper, which Guillermo had gone down for earlier. There was also a half-full cup of coffee with cream, toast and crumbs on a green plate, and a stick of partially melted butter that Guillermo had attacked without remorse. She also saw his cell phone. It was odd that he'd forgotten it since he was almost never away from the thing. They often talked about how much of his day he spent messaging his co-workers. In any event, she'd pour him a cup of coffee when he came home and then, if all was good with him, they'd go out to eat.

Surely they'd go to Santa María de Corrientes. It was a

restaurant only half a block from their apartment and they'd been there so many times she could picture it perfectly in her head: the walls decorated with photos, dolls, and other knickknacks. They liked the place, and would usually sit at a window seat in the corner, in front of the bus stop. Sometimes a bus would screech to a halt and she would cover her ears. On the longest wall, in the back of the restaurant, there were paintings, photographs, drawings, newspaper clippings, a pair of boxing gloves—dirty, and covered in dust, which Marina took note of every time she went to the bathroom—mirrors, and even bull horns. There were also little messages written on small chalkboards: *We Don't Serve Hot Water. No Credit Cards. No Credit, Only Cash.* "Just eat and be quiet," she would add, laughing, though Guillermo, absorbed in his own thoughts, would be looking the other way. Yes, just another Saturday.

Standing above the kitchen table, she fixed her gaze on Guillermo's phone, and then picked it up. The screen was scratched, and she could see her reflection in the dark glass: her eyes still swollen from sleep, little bags of darkness hanging under them; her hair a mess.

She sipped her coffee and touched the screen of the phone, turning it on. She was expecting to have to enter a password or some code, but instead she saw a long chain of chat messages from WhatsApp, along with the names of the people he'd been talking to in the last day.

She felt uncomfortable scanning the photos and names of Guillermo's contacts, but she couldn't help herself: there was Erlán, the teller one over from him at the bank; his mother Chichita; his brother Nacho; his lifelong friend Damián. There was also a good-looking woman in her early thirties who Marina didn't recognize—Silvana Fiorente was her name. There

were others as well, names and photos of friends and cowork-
ers she had either met or heard of: the account manager Ser-
gio Lamelia, a few other cashiers, and even the head of public
affairs, Mario Sufit.

Marina looked away; it was time to forget about the phone.
She'd never snooped on Guillermo before, or on anybody else.
Then she noticed how messy the living room was, and decided
to clean up as soon as she finished her coffee. Guillermo complained that she was so obsessive about things being neat, but
she knew that if it were up to him they would be eating junk
food surrounded by trash and dirty clothes—and so he should
be thankful. Tidy up, comb and feed the cat—she needed to
get to it. That couch loaded with last week's newspapers, piles
of clippings he'd cut out to save for who knows what, the beige
coat he'd left hanging over the chair that she needed to iron
again. And yet what stayed in her head was the photo of that
girl; she couldn't, she decided, *not* look at the chat conversation. Who was this Silvana Fiorente? If she was a fellow bank
employee they'd be talking about work, and she could forget
about it. She'd find some back-and-forth about numbers and
customers and she could then focus on her chores. She told
herself that it wasn't bad to dispel her doubt; plus, Guillermo
would never know.

She grabbed the phone again and opened to his chats.
She clicked on the little image of the blond-haired chick—
she was laughing in the photo, a strand of hair falling over
her face—whom Guillermo had been chatting with the night
before. The first thing Marina saw was a selfie: the woman
was in the dark, showing off her cleavage and staring into the
camera. Her hair (black in the photo) was down, her full lips
painted, her nose perfect. Underneath the photo, in the right
column, a small blue bubble: *You're going to kill me, Beautiful.*

The response was laughter.

Marina almost jumped. She moved her finger along the screen.

Another lethally boring day, he had written.

Sorry, my love, the woman responded. *Are you going to escape, or do I have to save you?*

He told her he was going to escape.

She dropped the phone onto the table. She felt her jaw tense, grinding her teeth. She walked to the window, opened it, and breathed in the fresh air. She felt overwhelmed. The cat came and rubbed its back against her leg, but she didn't even notice. She lifted her gaze and stared outside: it was an overcast Saturday. The sky, full of slate-gray clouds, looked ready to storm. From the sixth floor she could see the train station and the canopy of trees from the cemetery: big trees with long dark branches and leaves blowing, as if in slow motion, one way, and then the other.

She remembered that one night after checking Guillermo's pockets, she had stashed a packet of cigarettes in a drawer. She went to get the pack, lit a cigarette, and returned to the window.

Five minutes later she heard the key turning in the front door.

"Hi, Mari," Guillermo said, half-smiling. He carried a white envelope in his hand, and didn't have a pleasant look on his face.

She stayed at the window, the cigarette still burning. She flicked the butt out and peered at Guillermo, not opening her mouth.

"Did something happen?" he asked her.

"Nothing," she replied, turning to face the cemetery.

"Why the long face?"

She looked at him but didn't speak.

"I don't have great news," he said. He seemed worried, disheveled. "Dr. Lamotte is going to do an angiograph on Monday. There are some risks, but we need to do it. Until then: complete rest and no salt. Don't forget about the no salt."

Guillermo took off his black jacket and tossed it, as usual, onto the sofa. "He also gave me some Isordil pills," he said as he kicked off his shoes and left them next to the table, among the crumbs on the floor. "I need to slip one under my tongue if I start to feel bad."

She looked at his shoes, one on top of the other, and then turned back toward the window. She could hear the sounds of the street below. The salesmen hawking socks and cheap hats, the buses squealing to a stop at the corner, the calls and cries of children.

"Are you all right, love?" he asked, trying to hug her. He was pale and baggy-eyed, his lips cracked.

She didn't answer. She walked over to the sofa and sat down on top of his black jacket, crunching his reading glasses inside the pocket. She crossed her legs and wiped the crumbs off the bottom of her feet.

Guillermo seemed to be upset. He walked over to the sofa and grabbed his jacket by a sleeve, but Marina didn't budge.

"Excuse me." He tried to yank it from underneath her.

After another effort he was able to pull it out. Inside the pocket he found his glasses—a shattered lens and a broken frame. He laid his black jacket down next to his beige one.

"You forgot your phone," she said.

He scuttled quickly into the kitchen, found a rag, and went to the kitchen table, which he wiped down, moving his cup and a plate. He seemed to be looking for words. Next he went for a broom to sweep up the crumbs on the floor.

"I saw you were chatting with Fiorente. I guess you were trying to escape something."

Guillermo stopped cleaning and looked into her eyes. "It's just a work thing."

She smiled.

"What's with that dumb grin?" he asked.

She started to laugh.

"I don't want to fight now," Guillermo said. His forehead was suddening shining with sweat.

"All part of work, was it?" she guffawed.

"Stop it, love."

"I don't want to stop it." Marina dried her eyes, which were now tearing up from laughter. "So you're fucking around with that bitch."

"Calm down, please." Guillermo's face was getting redder and redder. His shirt was damp, plastered to his chest; he unbuttoned his collar. "I'm feeling funny." His face was wet now, his hands trembling. He tried to unbutton his shirt, but his fingers were fumbling. "Get me the Isordil," he said. "I'm really not feeling so hot."

She felt around in the black jacket, found and took out the pills, and then took two quick steps. When she was next to the window again, she looked out at the sky; it was darker than before. She leaned, held her arm out—the pill sleeve in her fist—and then she opened her fingers and let it fall. It followed the same arc as her cigarette butt. She glanced down at the sidewalk on Olleros Street.

"What are you doing, you psycho?"

Smiling, she turned toward Guillermo.

"Don't be stupid, forget about that girl."

"Sure thing," she responded. "Actually, I've already forgotten."

Guillermo closed his eyes hard, squeezed his lips together,

and brought his hands up to his chest. "Call someone. Call an ambulance."

Marina walked into the bathroom, came back out with a bottle of orange nail polish, sat down on the sofa, raised up a leg, and got herself comfortable to paint her toes.

"I feel really bad. Fuck. Get me my phone."

"Ask Fiorente. I'm busy." She raised the nail polish brush into the air.

"Don't do this to me, Marina. I can't move." Guillermo fell to his knees next to the sofa. He opened and closed his mouth like a fish out of water, and then started to cough, just like he had the night before.

"Bless you, love," Marina said.

Like she always did, she painted the toes on her right foot first. The big toenail took more time than any of the others, and she made sure to get the polish right up to the edge of her cuticle. Before she finished, she carefully tidied the edges.

The cat came up to inspect Guillermo, who had lain himself out on the floor. His eyes were reddening and he was breathing forcefully, in and out of his mouth. Marina jumped up, grabbed the landline, and then pulled the cord out. She went back to the sofa, took a deep breath, and shifted her attention to her left foot: it would take her another two or three minutes to finish the job.

"Orange is a pretty color," she said, as if she had just made an important discovery.

Guillermo started shaking slowly on the floor—as if his body were extremely heavy. That was when she got up and locked herself in the bathroom, just like she would when she was a girl.

She turned on the hairdryer. Drying her nails completely took about ten minutes. Then she did her makeup to cover

over how plain she was looking: a little blush on her cheeks, mascara on her eyelashes, and lipstick on her lips—something simple. She looked at herself in the mirror and impulsively decided that blond wasn't right for her anymore. She would set up an appointment with Ramón and dye her hair. She could do a deep chestnut, or even a black, like Silvana Fiorente. She left the bathroom and went into the bedroom where she put on a gray linen dress and black boots. Next she went to the kitchen to get the grocery cart. The cat came up to her stealthily, and then meowed, rubbing her back against Marina's leg, almost causing her to trip. She pushed it out of the way and went into the living room, toward the door. She had to step around Guillermo, who was still laid out next to the sofa.

"I'm going to head out to get some veggies to make you a soup. Or maybe not, maybe I'll get something delicious for myself. I've had a tough morning."

His gaze was locked on the far side of the room, his mouth half open. He wasn't moving.

In the lobby, Roberto the doorman was reading the paper behind his desk.

"How are you, Roberto?" Marina said. "I'm going shopping."

"To the market? I heard there are some new stalls."

"Just like every Saturday. I'm going to buy some good cheese and some mandarin liqueur. Guillermo's got a craving for it."

"He knows what's best."

Marina walked out into the street, turned, saw Roberto wave at her, and then hurried along the two blocks between her building and the market, which was in an old metal-roofed building next to the train station. She stopped outside to buy a pair of socks from a street vendor; she considered getting a pair of black panties too, but decided on beige instead, which was what she wore under her jeans in the winter.

An hour later she returned to her building, her cart full. As she walked to the elevator she said to Roberto: "I got that liqueur, and you wouldn't believe the avocados I found."

The doorman couldn't have imagined that, a few minutes later, Marina would be back, face contorted in horror, screaming: "Call an ambulance, Roberto! Guillermo is on the floor. He's in trouble! Please help me!"

Immediately, Roberto started to shake; he opened a drawer in his desk and shuffled some papers around. He tossed aside a few cards as he took out his cell phone and started dialing. "I'm calling the paramedics."

A moment later he explained to someone on the phone that there was a man in trouble, and then gave the address of the building. Marina heard him responding to a few brief questions. After he hung up, the two of them rode the elevator to the sixth floor. Marina stayed in the hallway, up against one of the walls. Roberto went into the apartment; seconds later he came back out, a serious look on his face.

"Let's go back downstairs," he said. "It will be better to wait there."

They rode back to the main floor. Soon, the ambulance pulled up and parked out front. Two men got out of the cab as Roberto opened the front door of the apartment building.

"I'm the doctor," the first man to walk into the building said. He wore a green smock and had a stethoscope hanging from his neck. The other man wore a blue smock and black plastic clogs on his feet.

"Are you the wife?" asked the man in green.

"Yes," Marina responded, "the wife."

"Let's hurry upstairs," he said.

The four of them got in the elevator together, nobody saying a word until the doors opened on the sixth floor. The apartment door was open; Guillermo was lying in the same spot she had left him in when she went to the market. The two men looked at each other, and then the doctor kneeled down. Without a word, he felt for Guillermo's pulse. The doctor checked his pupils, and then pressed the stethoscope to his chest for nearly a minute. Then he took Guillermo's hand and moved his fingers and wrist.

"I'm sorry," he finally said. "He's probably been dead for about an hour, given the rigidity of his hand."

Marina turned away, burying her face in her hands. She murmured that he must have died just after she'd left to go shopping. She explained that he had heart problems, and just that morning he was feeling bad and had gone to the hospital. But, she went on, she couldn't believe it. He hadn't seemed so terrible before she left.

The doctor and his assistant told her that you can't always see a heart attack coming, even with serious cases, and then they suggested that they move her husband onto the bed. Later, they assured her, people from the funeral home would come and take his body away.

Marina said that would be fine, and as the three men lifted Guillermo and took him to the bedroom, she went to the bathroom. Locked inside, she dried her face. Then she looked down at her toenails. She had missed a spot of polish on her big toe. She was annoyed, and felt like breaking something. She took out the bottle of orange polish and touched up her toes.

When she came out of the bathroom, the three men were waiting for her in the kitchen. They had her sign some paperwork. It started raining; the floor was getting wet in the living room, and she walked over to the window to close it.

When the three men went back downstairs, Marina reconnected the telephone cable. The cat watched her, but didn't meow. Marina opened the white envelope to read the results of the electrocardiogram. The report warned of severe arrhythmia, and confirmed a follow-up appointment for Monday. It was signed by Dr. Lamotte. She put the papers back in the envelope and, in a brusque motion, tossed the envelope onto the table. It would be important that Chichita and Nacho knew about Guillermo's latest medical news. She had to call them, as well as the people at the bank, to tell them what had happened. Everybody would want to go to his wake. She could wear her black dress with the little green dots, or maybe something else. On Monday she'd get the death certificate and plan for the burial, and then on Tuesday she could go to Ramón. She'd ask him to dye her hair, though she wouldn't tell him about Guillermo. Not yet. There'd be time for that later.

CHAMELEON AND THE LIONS

BY ALEJANDRO SOIFER

Palermo

Translated by M. Cristina Lambert

1

He buried his hands in the bucket of raw meat, and smelled a rotten steam rising from the bottom, which made him slightly dizzy. He touched the material: there were recently hardened pieces with brown bruises and crudely cut bones with splintered edges. He lifted the bucket, ten kilos of raw meat, and dragged it to the reinforced door. He placed the load on the ground, turned the handle that activated the gate catch, and opened it. The warm rays of an early spring morning sun crept into the bunker-like building.

He picked up the bucket with the animal food again and took some cautious steps toward the interior of the artificial habitat. It was one of the most spacious and best-cared-for cages in the Buenos Aires Zoo: a grass plateau with a small rectangular, shallow artificial lake that emulated the African savanna, with everything surrounded by a moat. It ended in a high wall from which visitors could see the beasts.

At a corner with exposed earth, where the grass covering had disappeared from so much traffic, he threw the food, and cautiously went to fetch the second, and then the third bucket of meat. He waited a moment, standing next to the small mound he had made, but none of the animals showed up to get their lunch.

He looked for the lions; two of them were sleeping in the shade of the acacia that rose near the cage's center, and next to them, the oldest one was licking some bones with its coarse tongue.

He was hot. The implacable midday sun bore down on him, through his security uniform. He wiped his forehead with the back of his gloved hand, sharpened his gaze, and saw it clearly: the old lion was consuming the remains of what looked like a human leg.

2

The blades of the ceiling fan moved the thick air in the small room where four men crowded together.

Rogelio Negrete, the lion keeper, couldn't stop sweating, and felt his arms shaking uncontrollably. His uniform reeked of vomit.

Detective Ernesto Camargo impatiently paced the small room surrounding an old dust-covered desk. He knew that the zoo director, that little bald guy with a head like a bowling ball and a carefully smoothed mustache, had brought them there to remove them from the center of attention.

"So, you came in, prepared to feed the lions, and discovered one of the animals eating the remains of a human being for breakfast?"

"Goldwyn, yes."

The detective arched his eyebrows.

"Goldwyn's the animal's name, sir," explained Inspector Mario Quiroz, who was observing the questioning while the forensic team collected evidence.

"And you didn't notice anything unusual when you arrived?"

"Nothing."

"Mr. Negrete has probably said all he has to say, don't you

think, detective?" interrupted the director. "If you'll allow me, I'd like to give this man the rest of the day off."

"Of course—after he makes a statement at the precinct. By the way, who was in charge of grounds security last night?"

"I'll have to check on that."

Quiroz did not like the director. He seemed anxious to get rid of them.

There were three knocks, and a policeman appeared at the half-open door. "We found something else," he announced.

The four men inside the room looked at each other.

"What're you waiting for, Quiroz? Go with Corporal Almirón and see what your men found," said the detective, visibly annoyed.

Quiroz followed the policeman, who led him through the lions' enclosure, where the animals had been locked up and drugged while the investigation was going on, to the open-air cage.

"Any idea who the poor devil was resting in the lion's stomach?"

"Not yet, sir."

The two men did not exchange another word. The corporal led Quiroz down a stone staircase from the plateau toward the moat, and then a few more steps to where the other investigators were gathered. Several camera flashes went off, and Quiroz made his way along until he stood before what had been discovered: surrounded by yellowish bovine bones was a human torso, its head showing lacerations from the animal bites. Faded black ink covered the upper part of what was left of an arm.

Quiroz crouched, covered his hand with the tip of his shirtsleeve, and moved the remains until the tattoo was completely visible. *"Kmaleon,"* Quiroz read the inscription out loud. "What the hell is this?"

3

"Do we know anything about the victim?"

"Only that he was alive when they threw him to the lions. He's still a John Doe. We didn't find any papers at the site, but he had a tattoo. It's only a matter of time until we find out who he was."

"What about the night watchman?"

"The guy on duty last night is named Vladimiro Olaya. He doesn't know anything."

"Are we sure, Quiroz?"

"I grabbed his balls with pliers and squeezed. I'm telling you, he didn't see anything. He must have been asleep when the crime took place."

Detective Camargo glared angrily at the inspector. Quiroz was known to be tough, a jerk, and Camargo had heard about his reputation as a son of a bitch in his youth with the Federal Police during the dictatorship; he wondered if Quiroz had indeed put pliers to the testicles of a witness and squeezed to make him talk. He could believe it. Quiroz could be sitting calmly at his desk talking to him, and five minutes later electroshocking someone in the precinct cellar. He was as changeable as a chameleon. That had been his nickname in the seventies: *Chameleon Quiroz.*

"I hope that poor bastard of a witness doesn't file a complaint against you."

The inspector hesitated a second before replying, and then said sarcastically: "A complaint? Against Mario 'the Iguana' Quiroz? Go back to your district attorney's office and get a statement from Olaya. I softened him up for you."

He hadn't been misinformed: Quiroz *was* a son of a bitch. But clearly he was also smart. At least smart enough to force everybody to call him *Iguana* instead of *Chameleon* when the Dirty War was over. That way, they would forget his past. He probably believed that.

"I'm assuming I can count on the good will of you and your people to solve this matter as soon as possible," said Camargo as he rose, and the two men walked to the front door of the precinct. "The election's in a month and . . ."

"Federal Homicide's at the service of your investigation, sir." And with that, Quiroz said goodbye and headed back to his office.

At the reception desk, a small, dark-skinned woman with long mahogany-colored hair was imploring an annoyed-looking officer with monotonous insistence and pompous hand gestures while she held out a photograph. Quiroz continued to his office, and was about to go in when he sensed there might be something in the photo the woman was showing the cop that he should check out. He retraced his steps to the reception desk.

"What's going on, miss?" Quiroz inquired. The officer at the reception desk could not disguise the relief on his face.

"I was explaining to the gentleman that I'm worried because my boyfriend disappeared last night."

"And I was explaining to her, sir, that we can't file a missing person report just because somebody was away from home for a few hours."

"Let me see that photo," Quiroz said, extending his hand.

The picture showed the woman herself with her arm around the waist of a guy much taller than her, with long hair down past his shoulders, wearing a frayed denim tank top and a word tattooed on his upper right arm; only the letters *Kma* could be seen. They were leaning against a red-and-white motorcycle with a River Plate sticker above the front light; they were at a park on a sunny day. The two lovers were smiling, happy and carefree.

"Miss, I have good news and bad news," said Quiroz drily. "The good news is I know where your boyfriend is. The bad news is he's in the morgue."

4

In the morgue, Gladys Ponce identified the remains recovered from the lions' moat as Daniel "Keys" Basualdo, keyboard player with the cumbia band Kmaleon.

Head almost severed, torso with the thoracic cavity exposed, with both arms (although the left one had been bitten off at the humerus) and the right leg. That was all there was, along with patches of skin, nerves, and muscles. The rest was a set of loose bones with torn, bloody tissue. It was all arranged as if it were a puzzle on Morgagni's metal table, under a white sheet that barely preserved whatever modesty remained of the gloomy find.

The woman burst into tears and Quiroz was tempted to embrace her, but quickly decided against it.

"It was my fault," she said between sobs while the policeman showed her the way out of the morgue. "I provoked him."

Quiroz searched his jacket pocket for the small black notebook he always carried, and as they walked down the cheerless corridor he casually asked the woman: "What do you do, Miss Ponce?"

"I'm from the province of Salta, sir. I've been living in Buenos Aires just a few months.

"That's fine, but please answer my question."

"I clean a house in Palermo," she sniffled, still crying.

"Why do you say it was your fault?"

"Oh, officer, Kmaleon played last night at the Metropolis Dance Club and I went to see them, as I do whenever I can. When the concert was over I met Daniel alone in the VIP room. He was acting strange, he was angry; he didn't like anything I said. He'd been really nervous for the past few weeks."

"Do you know what he was worried about?"

"No sir. I just wanted us to spend the rest of the night together, but he told me not to piss him off, and then we argued. I told him he no longer treated me like a queen, and he got mad and slapped me. I went home feeling awful. I waited for him all night; he'd sometimes show up after we fought. I thought after what he'd done to me he'd come by. But he never showed up. Today I went looking for him at his house, and didn't find him. None of his friends knew where he was; I got worried, had a bad feeling, and went to the police station. You saw the rest."

They left the building.

"You'll have to come back to the station with me," the inspector said. "I need you to make a formal statement."

5

Quiroz got out of the car and stepped onto the dirt road. There was a Peronist party banner stretched across the width of the block. The cop passed beneath it with indifference. He had never voted, and never would. *Democracy is a perverted system for the weak-hearted.*

Cyan, the record label that Kmaleon recorded for, was located in the only two-story house in the area, with a flower bed in front and an electric gate. The rest were small, modest properties packed with families; many of the structures were bare brick or had whitewashed walls.

He rang the bell and waited at the gate. A woman in an apron opened the door, Quiroz announced himself, and the woman disappeared inside again. He waited until the electric gate opened and continued up the short flagstone pathway. The front door opened again, and the maid led him inside, through a corridor, and down a staircase to the garage.

The space was divided by a glass cubicle surrounded by cement walls, and on the other side seven musicians were playing, crowded together. The song ended and everyone relaxed, laid their instruments on the floor, and cracked open cans of beer. A guy in a jacket, dress pants, and a tieless white shirt came out of the recording booth. He wore his hair flattened back with gel; it looked wet.

"Alberto Montero. How can I help you, Officer Quiroz? Is it about Keys? We already gave a statement to the detective."

"We'd better go to your office, if you don't mind."

The guy, displaying his hairy chest behind a gold chain with a huge cross through his unbuttoned shirt, led the way into the booth.

The space was larger than it appeared, and beyond the recording console was a table that served as a desk with two chairs. To one side, against a wall plastered with cumbia band posters, a gawky kid was copying CDs on a computer. A cardboard box next to him already held a pile of pirated discs. A photocopier on his right kept spitting out record jackets, with the original label's logo crudely erased—*Unstoppable*, by the band The New Cream.

"Don't stop, Jonathan. I'll be talking with the gentleman, but you keep on copying and packing, as we have to distribute the merchandise."

The two men silently sized each other up for a moment.

"Now, how can I help you?" Montero said.

"As you figured, I came about Keys."

Montero closed his eyes and nodded. "A terrible thing. The other band members happen to be here, and I'd like to introduce you to Braian Ayala, the leader." He picked up a microphone from his desk and called, "Chimp, come here, a policeman wants to talk to you."

Moments later a young man entered.

"You're the leader of Kmaleon?"

"Yes sir."

"You know what happened to Daniel Basualdo?"

"Yes sir; Alberto here told me about it. We already spoke to the detective and told him everything that happened Sunday night."

The musician couldn't have been more than twenty-seven, and he wore his long, curly hair down to his waist. A medal of the Virgin Mary hung from his neck, and he had on worn-out jeans and a denim tank top, identical to the one Quiroz had seen on the victim in Gladys Ponce's photo. In fact, he too had *Kmaleon* tattooed on his arm. They could have been brothers, but in fact it was the band look that Montero had designed. The rest of the band dressed and looked the same as well.

"Basualdo's girlfriend says he seemed nervous Sunday night after the concert you played."

"Keys was a little messed up. He rarely hung out with the boys and he missed lots of rehearsals."

"Any idea why he was upset?"

"No sir."

"What did you do after the concert?"

"We had a party with the band and some groupies in one

of the Metropolis VIP rooms," the manager explained.

"And Basualdo was there?"

"No, Keys left with Gladys," the young musician replied, "and after that nobody else saw him. We asked him to come to the party, but he wanted nothing to do with it."

Quiroz smelled lies in the air. And sensed that Montero was not totally trustworthy. "Very well, thank you for your time."

"Was nothing, officer. By the way, you know who you're voting for?" Montero asked, standing up at the same time as Quiroz.

"No."

"Let me give you a ballot in case you vote in the city. My brother's running for congress as a Peronist."

Annoyed, Quiroz took the ballot and put it in his pants pocket.

6

"I know you've been making inquiries on your own in that kid's case, the one in the cumbia band, Quiroz."

"I just questioned a few witnesses."

"I don't like things happening outside of what this office dictates."

"What's the matter with you? Why so nervous?"

"You're not going to screw me, Quiroz. Just do as you've been told," said Detective Camargo before hanging up the phone.

Three knocks on the door caught Quiroz by surprise. It was Almirón; he always knocked the same way.

"Come in, asshole."

"I'm sorry, sir, but I think you should see what's happening on TV right now," said Almirón, and when his boss nodded he turned on the old TV with a worn-out cathode tube that displayed images in diluted colors with a purplish hue. He went quickly through the channels until he stopped on Report TV announcing in huge letters: *CUMBIA BUSINESSMAN RIDDLED WITH BULLETS.*

Quiroz settled uncomfortably in his chair and let out an annoyed sigh. Anselmo Ramírez, captain of the 42nd Precinct, appeared on the screen. They had been partners commissioned at the same time, but had not spoken in a while.

"After receiving a report at police headquarters from a neighbor about gunshots, we went to the victim's home, where we found the front door had been forced open," Ramírez intoned with a policeman's cadence, while on screen they showed various images of the victim's bloody body. "We went inside the residence, and on the living room floor found a lifeless male with ten large-caliber bullet holes. The victim has been identified as Romeo Portillo. According to statements from witnesses and next of kin, Portillo managed cumbia bands."

"Turn that shit off, will you?"

"Another murder in the cumbia scene."

"It makes no difference; the detective doesn't want us to move our ass without his supervision. Leave, Almirón, just go."

The corporal nodded and left the office.

Quiroz rose from the chair, grabbed his overcoat, and went out into the overcast afternoon.

He walked at a leisurely pace down Santa Fe Avenue toward Pacific Bridge and went inside Kentucky Pizzeria on Godoy Cruz Avenue. It was six thirty in the evening and there, in a back corner, was Héctor "Fats" Argañaraz, leaning on the table that had been specially reserved for him for decades, and where he carried out his dirty dealings to the pace of the *fugazzeta* pizza slices ceaselessly passing before his eyes. Quiroz wondered how a man could eat so much cheese pizza without his heart exploding. No matter the time, from five in the afternoon until well past dawn, anyone who went by could see Argañaraz wolfing down slice after slice. In any case, the black spots on his neck were a sign of pancreas failure: the policeman knew diabetes or a heart attack were not far off for the big ball of grease known as Fats.

"Fats." The cop approached the obese man, who shoved a slice of pizza into his mouth, dried the oil from his hands on a paper napkin, and extended one in welcome.

"How can I help you, officer?" Fats pointed to a chair in front of him. His voluminous belly pressed against the edge of the table, so that there was always a bit of distance between him and his visitors. Quiroz was grateful: Fats's onion breath could knock out a horse. A new cheese-and-onion slice seemed to drop from the sky in front of the man.

"There was a party in the VIP room at the Metropolis Club on Sunday."

"Sunday?"

"Spare me, and don't pretend you don't know what I'm talking about."

Fats smiled. "You know I'd like to cooperate with the very noble institution you represent, but lately I've been hearing a lot of complaints from my girls. They tell me they're being robbed in the neighborhood and harassed. The other day, a new little girl I have, top quality, her name's Loli—she's twenty, but looks sixteen—a degenerate roughed her up, beat the shit out of her actually, and left without paying. They laughed like hell at us in your precinct."

"You want me to go after a guy who fucked one of your whores and didn't pay?"

"And hit her," replied Fats, running the edge of his hand over his shiny lips.

Quiroz thought it over for a second. "I'll see what we can do," he grumbled, "but you'll have to help me."

"Gladly. I love cooperating with my friends." Fats signaled to the guy at the register to send him another slice.

"Yeah, right. Stop being such an ass."

"I only heard what they're saying in the neighborhood. They took transvestites to the party."

"None of yours?"

Fats's face turned into a twisted red grimace. "Officer, I thought you knew I don't work with homosexuals. Go talk to those dimwits who're stealing my clientele."

Quiroz rose from the table.

"Listen, officer, what about my problem?"

"Come by the station tomorrow and we'll see." He left the pizzeria while Fats stuffed the last *fugazzeta* bite into his mouth.

7

Quiroz went up Godoy Cruz Avenue where he found some cross-dressers standing by their informal posts against the thick walls of the San Martín railroad station. He approached a group of two—one short, chubby-cheeked, and dark in a silver wig, the other a little taller, also dark but scrawny. Both wore very low-cut tops that emphasized their cheap breast implants and fishnet stockings that squeezed the flesh of the short, chubby one.

"This is the time when kids come home from school," he addressed them harshly. "Couldn't you at least cover up your pathetic show till nightfall?"

The tall cross-dresser responded with disgust: "And who

are you to tell us how to dress? Get out of here, wanker."

The short one elbowed her. "Candy, you jerk, he's the fuzz."

"Is what my friend Yoselin says true? You're a pig? Don't try screwing with us; we already paid for protection this week."

"Calm down, darlings, I'm here on a strictly official matter."

"You all say the same thing, and we end up having to service you behind a tree so you'll leave us alone," Candy said.

"Don't worry; before I let you stick your cock in my ass I'll rip it off and cram it down your throat." Quiroz leaned back against the railroad station wall calmly, pulled a cigarette from his overcoat, and lit it.

"If you didn't come to fuck, what did you come for?"

A black car with tinted windows accelerated when it passed in front of the trio.

"You're ruining our business!" shouted Candy. "That guy *always* picks us up!"

"All the more reason for you to help me. You talk, I leave, and you continue working. What do you think of the deal?"

Candy sighed, exhausted. "Tired of the abuses from you people. *TIRED*. That's what I think."

Quiroz leaned toward Yoselin: "Will this go better if I talk to you?"

The short, chubby transvestite nodded sadly. "What do you want from us?"

"Private party last Sunday at the Metropolis. Who was there?"

Yoselin turned pale.

"Why are *you* interested in that?" Candy asked.

"What the hell do you care why it interests me? Were you there or not?"

"We weren't," said Yoselin finally, "but we know someone who was. She's been in hiding since Monday."

Quiroz blew cigarette smoke into the short transvestite's face. "Now we're getting somewhere. You know what name the witness goes by and where she's staying?"

"Giselle," Candy said after a moment.

"They say she's at the Old Man's house."

"See? Cooperating makes everything easier."

The Old Man's house was a hideout two blocks away. It was an old, half-finished building without glass in the windows and facing the street. Quiroz saw a dim light coming from the second floor. He went through the open, dented sheet-metal door, climbed the stairs, dodging a junkie lying on the steps halfway up, and kicked open the door where the light was coming from.

A transvestite with runny makeup was resting on a thin and filthy mattress, a wig next to her on the floor, reeking of cheap alcohol and dirt. "Who is it?" she whispered, barely opening her eyes.

"Santa Claus! Merry Christmas!" Quiroz replied and approached the transvestite, who sat up on the mattress with difficulty.

"Whatever you want, but don't shout, love."

"This'll be short," said the policeman, opening his overcoat to show the 9 mm Beretta 92FS at his waist. "What happened at the last party for Daniel 'Keys' Basualdo, a musician with Kmaleon?"

The cross-dresser took a furtive look at the glassless window on her right and tried to make a dash for it. Quiroz tackled her just as she was about to jump from the second-floor window. He grabbed her by the armpits, and dangling her body in space told her: "If I let you go, you'll fall on your head and crack open your skull. I don't think you want to die today."

"It wasn't me!" Giselle cried.

"So what happened?"

"They hired me and other girls," she panted. "They told us it was a party with the whole band in the VIP room. And that it would go on until three in the morning. Then they grabbed me and took me to another private room, just the manager, the singer, and Keys. I was with the three of them, and when we finished they started to argue."

"What did they argue about?"

"I don't know!"

"Think, damnit!" Quiroz shook the transvestite while she hung over the void.

"Something about leaving the band, going to another label—Keys was tired of the piracy. He used that word."

"Then?"

"The vibe got heavy, and they told me to leave. I went back home and found out the next day on the news what happened to him. I got real scared, and I've been hiding here ever since."

Quiroz pulled her back inside and left the dump.

8

The recording room walls no longer shook with sonic vibrations, and only a few instruments lay on the floor. It was nearly midnight when Quiroz stormed in.

"Montero, I know you're here, come out, damnit!" he shouted, brandishing the Beretta.

The manager peeked out from behind the glass booth, saw the cop, and smiled. He opened the door to the room and let Quiroz in. Against the wall, next to the PC that continued to burn pirated records, the front man and leader of Kmaleon,

Braian "Chimp" Ayala, was smoking a joint very calmly, as if a policeman wasn't pointing a gun at them.

"Officer, you know we welcome you here, no need for such a dramatic entrance."

"Shut up, you piece of shit," Quiroz snapped. Still aiming the pistol, he groped for the Nokia hooked to his belt. "Both of you, on your knees, hands behind your heads where I can see them."

"What's with this jerk?" Chimp said, as if just waking up from a nap.

"It's a game. Come on, do as the officer says and we'll laugh about it later."

"Shut your mouth or I'll blast you," Quiroz said, while punching numbers into his Nokia and still pointing his weapon. Camargo finally answered.

"Detective Camargo, excuse me for bothering you at this late hour, but I've solved the Keys Basualdo case. I'll wait here with the two suspects for you to make the collar. Hurry." He gave him the address and hung up. He sat down in Montero's office chair.

"So? Now what?"

"Now we wait for the detective."

"This is gonna be fun," said Montero.

The next twenty minutes were interminable for Quiroz, who nevertheless remained calm, silencing his suspects with his pointed gun whenever they tried to exchange a word. Detective Ernesto Camargo finally arrived at the recording studio. He wore a serious and tired expression; he seemed to have aged ten years in the past week, last time the cop had seen him.

"Here I am. Can you tell me why the hell you got me out of bed? And what are you doing with these men?"

"Ernesto Camargo, how are you, dear?" Montero greeted him, still on his knees.

"Shut up, Alberto, this isn't the time."

"I called you, detective, because here I have Daniel 'Keys' Basualdo's killers, the ones who threw him in the lions' cage. And I'm sure they're also involved in the murder of Romeo Portillo, another impresario."

"What nonsense is this, Quiroz? Alberto Montero's an old acquaintance of mine, very respectable, and I won't allow—"

"Early Sunday morning, after the Kmaleon concert, the band had a party at the Metropolis," Quiroz began. "Keys Basualdo didn't go right away; first he was with his girlfriend Gladys Ponce. They had a tense encounter, they argued. Basualdo, according to Ponce, had been very nervous the last few weeks. And that night the conflict blew up. After his girlfriend left, Keys joined the party in the VIP room with the rest of the band, and stayed until nearly three in the morning. Then Montero, Ayala, Basualdo, and a transvestite who goes by the name of Giselle went to a private room. The four of them continued partying there, but these two knew they had to get rid of Basualdo. Why? Because Keys was fed up with Kmaleon and their manager. Montero traffics in pirated CDs by other cumbia bands. He set up a series of fake recording labels to sell the pirated copies through newspaper and magazine kiosks. This eventually caused a problem for Basualdo, and he decided to get out—"

"Keys was a jerk," Montero cut in. "He was part of the deal, but he was a pussy. He had too many scruples. He said we were screwing other bands by ripping them off, that a friend of his, the Trinidadian singer, had lost his job because of our business. All because of copying and distributing some pirated records."

"So they killed him."

"The imbecile was talking about joining another band led by Portillo. We was never a straight arrow, but at least his shady dealings didn't affect the 'cumbia family,' as that idiot Keys used to say."

"Sometime that night they started arguing again and threw out the transvestite. Basualdo must have been totally wasted by then. They suggested going for a walk, to get some fresh air. They knew the zoo guard always fell asleep. Maybe they even used to walk around the zoo every night after the concerts—an irresistible attraction. Keys, who was completely drunk, couldn't offer much resistance. They threw him into the lions' cage and you know the rest of the story. Am I wrong?"

"That's more or less how it happened. Only that the business about the sleeping guard came as a surprise. We decided to go that way to get rid of him because as we walked through the Palermo Woods where we'd planned to put a bullet in his head, we saw the guard was asleep. Chimp's idea," Montero said, caressing the back of his neck.

The other one barely responded; he simply offered a look of stoned satisfaction.

Detective Camargo scratched the space between his eyebrows with his index finger. "Very cute little story, Quiroz. Now go home and stop busting my balls."

"What?"

"You heard me. Get the hell out of here."

"But aren't you going to arrest them?"

The detective took two steps toward Quiroz. "Listen to me, you nincompoop. Didn't I tell you I didn't want you to go over my head? Now you're going to listen to me, whether you want to or not. This guy you have on his knees is the brother of a big shot in the nightclub union who is also a future congressman. You really want to risk your miserable life for this? For some nobody who ended up as lion feed? Don't be a jerk, Chameleon. Shed your skin once more as you do so well, and go home to your wife."

Quiroz was still aiming his gun at the suspects. Montero smiled and slowly began to get up.

"You heard the detective, Chimp, let's go, it's over."

The policeman slowly lowered the gun and put it in its holster. He felt outraged and stunned. Camargo slapped him on the back. "Go home."

Quiroz began to retrace his steps. He left like a boxer who had just taken a tremendous beating.

"You see, officer," Montero said behind him, "killing a guy in this country and getting away with it is a piece of cake. Cake eaten by lions."

Then he heard peals of laughter, though nothing mattered to him anymore that night.

PART III

Imperfect Crimes

THE GOLDEN ELEVENTH

BY GABRIELA CABEZÓN CÁMARA

Barrio Parque

Translated by John Washington

You look out the window at the flowing path of the highway, smooth like a river, the highway down below golden in the same light that falls on you, on the golden cars almost lost in the light of the highway, just there and yet still so far from the exhaust in your head, Ariel. You see it like a line twisting on itself, opening, splitting, beautiful in this light so far below your room, the highway silent at this distance, which isn't really so far but as far as you've come for now. Soon you're going to be gone, far away, so far, Ariel, that you might even miss this place, but really you won't miss shit, you think, as you keep looking down. You better start planning on new heights after spending hours looking down from the eleventh floor you've risen to: you've climbed, Ariel, all the way up to here, all the way up to this table with its line of amber-white powder, clean, the line of amber as if floating on the designer glass table. You're happy in your bubble, concentrating on your work under the light, you've been living two days illuminated on the eleventh floor, and the clean and crystal highway golden like the line of coke on the table, floating on your own reflection, you see it as if weightless and suspended over itself in its smooth amber white, as if you were tromping through and catching little glimpses of ghosts in the Arctic, where you might be heading soon, where you might want to visit. Why not? It's got to be clean, Alaska, with its pines and its ferocious hairy dogs pulling sleds. You're going to steer your sled from up so high, red and yellow shooting across the ice after the dogs; and you'll marry a white girl and you'll live with her in the woods close to a little village, and you'll chop down beautiful pine trees for Christmas even though you live in a forest, and what would you need to cut down a tree for? You don't want to kill anything, not a single other thing, not even a tree: you'll hang ornaments on the tree closest to the house so the colored lights shine in the whiteness. Is it really white? Is snow actually white? White like a sheet of paper before writing or white like the amber-white powder floating on itself, levitating on the table, enjoying its moment of weightlessness until it's snorted? Waiting for you like your new Victorinox knife you bought for the trip, red with its white cross, right next to the silver Zippo, everything dry and bright at this height, Ariel, dry and clean and in order. You've gotten yourself ready, it was hardly anything, just what you bought for the trip, your new clothes: underwear, shirts, jeans, all brand-name—everything from the Alcorta mall. They were a little nervous when they saw you walk in, they eyed you, but then you put on their clothes and you walked out of there like a gentleman and the thugs didn't even recognize you. You weren't from the barrio anymore, they asked you for some change to buy a beer and you gave it to them and then went to buy your own German beer in Malba. And you thought, *Yes, like this, more or less, this place full of plazas and museums where they treat you like a king would treat you in some foreign country.* Aaaah, yes, like this, like in a movie, strutting down the New York streets, you're going to start going for morning runs in Central Park because that's how you live a good life, waking up early before work to run, even if you're the president. But no, no, not the president, he lives in Washington and he's black and you're not, which is why you get to leave, because you're not black, not like the rest of them, you don't belong, you've been wanting to leave since you were born, which is why you're going to get up and run and drink coffee from a mug out on the street in the middle of winter. Even when it's snowing you're going to take off your gloves and warm your hands on your coffee mug while the steam billows out of your mouth; and you're going to stroll around like you're in the movies, and you're going to stay away from the gangs. You'll be alone in New York, you're going to start over, this is the last job you're going to do and they're not going to catch you. You're going to live easy now. What luck you never got tattooed like everyone else, just the Nazi cross that you have over your heart. You're going to have to work someday, you explained to them, but you'll always be one of them, those who saved you from the prison tomb where you almost became the wife of the black thug of thugs, but not you, you're the white-collar hacker, which is what you studied so hard in prison for. The ace in the sleeve of the Aryan South Americans when the bullets or the knives don't do the trick. You've always been primed for something better—you knew it, and they knew it, and now there is your little suitcase with everything you need, the clothes folded like your mom taught you, a photo with her and your sister, just one photo, because everyone else in your life disappeared with every phone you lost or broke or every computer that met the same fate and died; all the other photos gone now, and they're gone too, your mother and sister, in a shoot-out with the Peruvian narcos, asshole sons of bitches. Those sorry motherfuckers will see now, but what a shame you won't get to see their faces when the metal rains down. But what metal? There's not going to be any metal, and you don't want to think of this now, you just want to know that your mother and sister, wherever they are, are proud of you, that you're here breathing in that purified air on the eleventh floor of that seven-star mega hotel doing your work, though they probably wouldn't approve of the work you're doing now. Your mom didn't break her back so you could be a crook, poor lady, cleaning the houses of rich folk who live just around the corner from where you are now. They let her in because she was light-skinned, even though she was from the barrio and they sensed that she had lived a tragedy: an injustice, a fall from grace; white people aren't born into the barrio, they fall into it and always know that they're not from there just like you always knew it. Your mom who took you to school every morning of your life and sat with you and your sister every night to go over homework, you could almost cry, but you can't work like this. You stop to go to the bathroom, that beautiful marble you've been living with for the last few days, you wash your face and look in the mirror and you like what you see, it fits you, the mirror and frame and marble and haircut and shave and soft cotton of the shirt that shines a little bit, it all bodes a bright future, all of it, Ariel. Stay calm, you're going to be just one more foreigner so you have to concentrate now. Maybe it's time to cool it with the lines of amber-white powder floating in that light like the sun that is already lowering over the shithole barrio, and you pause, you feel remorse, that you've left now, that you're so far away though you can see it through the window all twisted in broken lines, one house on top of another without any foundation. It's almost a miracle they don't fall apart as if God wanted us to live all piled on top of each other, as if lines couldn't be straight, as if nature itself were against a clean line. The sacks of shit who first built one on top of another for the families spilling out as if they were looking to actually live a life; those sad shits living and breathing exhaust billowing off that awful highway that when seen from down below isn't clean and full of light like you see it from above: from below the highway is a dark sewer swirling with exhaust and oil and trash thrown by the sons of bitches driving cars, flying from one place to another, looking down at the barrio on the side of the road for two minutes at ninety miles an hour. From here the highway is beautiful, and the barrio too, and it makes you a little sad that you see its beauty only from afar, from another place, when you're already gone, with the barrio about to fall to pieces because it's going to crumble and people are going to die tonight because that beautiful highway is going to fall right on top of the barrio even though they told you it wouldn't, that if anybody dies it will only be by accident, that they just wanted the people to move, to shake their twisted towers of trash. Maybe it's true or maybe you're just imagining this craziness because you're leaving and in leaving you feel sympathy for the crooked houses and shit-stacks held together by a miracle. Looking down and now feeling shame again, thinking of Arno and Jennifer, who loved you even though you always told her she wasn't going to be your wife because you were going to leave that place and you weren't going to be able to bring her with you, because you didn't want to be from the barrio so you couldn't marry a black piece of shit like her even if she loved you. And she did love you, but you never told her this and you left her and left Arno, your little dog Arno who took care of you when that thing happened with your sister and your mom; Arno who licked you when you cried and who curled up next to you when you couldn't sleep, turning over and over. Arno who accompanied you when you went for your runs or who barked at Jenny, Arno who understood and went out to rescue you in the rain even when the whole barrio outside was just a swamp of mud and shit. You're going to shit, with the light from the window flashing on the line of powder. Get it off that floating mirror, stop it from flashing at you, and cut a line. Make it as beautiful as the highway now—yes, that's better, cut it in two, good thing you bought the Victorinox, which cuts a line for you all the way to the north, to the river, to the delta, which keeps you straight and fills your head with that golden light that seems to pause there above, between the highway and heaven, in your head here on the eleventh floor. High-quality product you're filling yourself with and cold light and once again you think of Alaska and the white woman, yes, what you're in the mood for, a white woman, right now, you could just call one up and your cock stiffens looking at the book that was left for you in which a number of extremely pale blond chicks look back at you from the cover. They told you you could spend as much money as you wanted. You checked on your computer but you haven't figured out where so much money was coming from—$250,000 to spend. All you have to do is finish the work now, so you make a call for a blonde like the one who's making you as hard as a baseball bat, as you like to think; you're ready to take her hard as a pole like a gringo on vacation to La Paz, you just need a little more time to put the circuits in order, to get ready to activate, ready for the command to make it fall naturally, at the exact moment they decide to press the button, whoever *they* are. It doesn't matter to you. There's a bunch of them there today. You were trying to see at breakfast if there were others like you new to this life, living in the most expensive hotel in Buenos Aires, with a view of the river and the tracks and the barrio that's going to shit. You chop another little line for yourself but you better go slow, this powder is like a venom—

the purest product, the whitest white, even though it's amber white, as if they bathed it in the light of a jungle at dawn, and not in the miserable kitchens where they actually produce the powder. You keep working, looking up now and again at the computer screen and the reddening sun out the window, almost all the way fallen now on this day when so much else will fall. And now you're done and you deserve a big line, and you make it into a trembling zigzag to resemble the piece-of-shit houses and you laugh and pour yourself a glass of eighteen-year-old Dalmore that was put in the room along with the coke and the book of blond girls. Yes, they know how to treat somebody, how gorgeous they are. You take a swig and think that it was all worth it; you've never drank anything so good and you ask yourself why not just go to Scotland? All there is to do now is wait for the Aryans to bring you a passport that will let you travel to the US and England, wherever your sweet ass feels like throwing down another line of coke and having another drink of that golden whiskey, as if you were drinking the sun, the glowing highway—you toast the sky. *Look, Mom, I'm drinking the same drink your grandpa would drink. My dear mother, we've arrived. Look at me, Mom.* One more line and you're hard and as indestructible as the Tower of London. You'd like to stick it in a blonde, look at your Big Ben and she deep-throats and looks up at you with those eyes bugging out with so much cock in her mouth. You open the book of blondes and your dick keeps growing bigger and bigger than it's ever been and you call the concierge of the hotel and you tell him to send Barbie up to you. He tells you that she's busy and you tell him to stop fucking around and send up the blondest blonde he can find or he can come up and suck your dick himself or you're going to come down and stick him like he's a chicken over a fire. And the guy laughs and tells you to give him fifteen minutes and you prick up even more and you tell him to get on it or else, and you know you have to come down a little or you're going to end up strung out and alone on the bed. But you cut yourself another line and open the computer to try to figure out where all the money is coming from or who's making the devices. You look around and try to figure out what the hell you've gotten yourself into but you find nothing at all. You note that the devices, twenty of them, are all under the highway along the shithole barrio and you ask yourself if the high-frequency sound waves that are going to scream out will indeed activate one of those bombs that cause enormous explosions. They told you that it's not, it's just going to crack the columns holding up the highway, which would be enough to have to evacuate the shithole barrio and demolish the whole thing, which couldn't be, but why not? If they're going to pay you $250,000, you know they aren't paying you for anything good and it's certainly no good to knock over an entire highway and you serve yourself another whiskey and someone knocks on your door and you open it nervously and see this phenomenal woman and you think that with so much beauty nothing bad could happen in the world and you unzip your fly and her eyes widen and she tells you that she has never, never, *nunca* in her life seen anything like that big daddy. And then she asks if you're a porn star and you tell her to cut it with the bullshit and you start ripping off her clothes and she tells you that it's going to cost you, that you've just added a thousand bucks for tearing her blouse, and then she realizes that for someone like you a little extra money is a drop in the bucket and you have her there in front of you and you tell her to shut it and she takes you into her mouth and you've never before had a blonde kneeling in front of you and you look down at her hair, her white ears, and you choke her a little and fill her mouth with jizz and she swallows. And you know she'll charge you for that too but you don't care and you make her walk over naked and you cut a couple lines and you fuck her but you can't concentrate anymore. You're thinking of the noise you're going to hear when the fuses blow; it's not going to be slow. You think the whole shithole will go up in flames. They told you that where the barrio is now, they're going to build a paradise and you think that, yes, this is it, you always knew that nobody was going to dupe you. That you couldn't have kids with her because black genes are always passed down and you're not going to raise little black babies, but what the fuck? You should have taken Jenny up here, you could have at least fucked her here and you could have tied her tubes, the goddamn whore, *You damn whore, get out of here!* you yell at the blonde who tells you, *Okay, no problem, very nice to meet you.* But you have to pay her now so you throw down some bills and she has to squat to get them. She tells you you're a drug addict son of a bitch and you can go to hell and you shove her nearly naked into the hallway, you throw her shirt out to her and you get dressed and cut another line and put a baggy in your pocket and you pocket the black credit card and think that you could take Arno to Alaska as well. You go downstairs and tell the concierge that if anybody is looking for you, you'll be back in ten minutes, and you start running and realize that a car is following you and you're scared and you call Jenny while still running and tell her to get out of the barrio, to run to Retiro and to take Arno with her. You tell her to go, to take the route she always takes, and the people in the car are slowly getting closer like they're letting you get all the way to the barrio. It's time now. They stop and you keep running and you know that if the sons of bitches are stopping it's because it's safer to stop because what you installed is about to blow, but you keep running away from the hotels, now you cross the next block into the barrio and you see Jenny coming toward you with Arno behind her, beelining directly to you, and he jumps up and licks your face as if he knew that you had almost left him for good and you run to Jenny and grab her by the hand and pull her and she doesn't understand but follows you because that's how Jenny is, and the alarm on your watch sounds and you run faster and you don't stop, never again will you stop. You leave flying at five hundred kilometers an hour and you're not able to see the orange of the explosion because it knocks the three of you against one of the columns supporting the highway. You're only able to hug both of them and think that you saved them and remember the face of the gringo, the boss of the boss of the bosses of the Aryans from the prison tomb. He was a Nazi like you, but whiter, he worked as a mercenary to the best bidder, sure, sure, the money that you didn't get a chance to spend was from the furniture shops that they built in other cities, razed to the earth, just like they razed the barrio. You hug them, Ariel, you melt, embraced in the orange light of the explosion. They are all dead, Ariel.

ETERNAL LOVE

BY ERNESTO MALLO

Barrio 11

Translated by John Washington

One merely has to walk around Barrio 11, the Jewish neighborhood of Buenos Aires, on any day after the businesses have shuttered their windows and the sidewalks are left flooded with discarded cloth, cardboard rolls, paper, and trash thrown out by the merchants and peddlers, to find themselves with the men, women, and children who sift through this waste, fishing for materials they can sell by the pound to recycling sites. These people survive by digging through garbage. Primarily benefiting from this misery are the police officers who collect their hush money, not in exchange for protection, but just for a momentary looking-the-other-way, an unreliable permission to go on. The rich Jewish families have started their slow and continuous exodus from the neighborhood, and though they're keeping their businesses in Barrio 11, they're starting to prefer living in Barrio Norte or Belgrano, residential areas that offer greater social prestige. The once luxurious buildings of the golden age are now filled with old people whose fortunes have been poured into high-rise apartments around the Libertador Gardens, vacations to Punta del Este, private, supposedly British schools, and imported cars.

Pablo Maese couldn't care less. He's happily walking down Sarmiento Street, having just received the good news at the Ministry of Culture that he'll be commissioned to build a statue of Eva Perón, to be erected in the Rubén Darío Plaza. When the work is unveiled, they will call it *Evita*. The minister told him this in person. On top of the commission, they'll also give him a work studio, and he'll be able to hire three assistants and a model to help him with his magnum opus. His next few months are secure. He has won the tug-of-war with Gianetti, his rival sculptor, and now the first step is to put to paper the monument he's already been sketching in his head. It'll be a composition in which Eva, cast in bronze, will reflect maternal sweetness, lightly positioning, as if she were fearful of hurting it, an ethereal right hand on the head of a boy in a group of children tangling themselves in the layers of her dress. To her left, a solid mass of laborers, inspired by those that Carpani drew, a cluster of muscle and resistance. But he'll keep this point of inspiration subtle, because he's unsure to which end of the Peronist spectrum the ministry is now leaning. Either way, this will be a young, vibrant, sensual Eva, yes, but also a humble Eva—sweet but fierce—an angel who can wield a flaming sword. He'll give her an objective, precise gaze, like Michaelangelo gave to David. The metal of her dress will reflect the movement of the wind, like in Sorolla's beachside paintings. He sees it, in his mind he sees it, amongst springtime flowering jacarandas, framed by the National Library in the background, erect, dignified, brilliant, young: the true heroin of the shoeless.

He's thinking of all this when he sees her. She's picking through the trash that's being laid out before her by an old, obese, and clumsy-mannered woman. The beauty of the girl's form is apparent even underneath her grime and rags. The old woman turns sharply to him.

"What's going on? You like the girl?"

Pablo turns slowly toward the old woman, but doesn't take his eyes off the girl. Only when he has completely turned do his eyes peel away from her and land on the old woman. If he ever wanted to paint or draw a witch, here was the perfect model. Big-nosed, with hairy warts on her forehead and cheeks, yellow, scrambled teeth, and narrow, watery eyes. Scola's film, *Ugly, Dirty & Bad*, comes immediately to mind. *What an inspiring, rejuvenating day*, he thinks. *The cosmos seems to be working in my favor*. He smiles at the women.

"You want to make a few pesos?"

The witch flashes him a broken smile, but her eyes are not laughing, they're calculating. "It's always nice to have the possibility of earning some pesos through honorable work," she replies.

Pablo smiles, and thinks honor must seldom be practiced in this woman's life. Under her covetous gaze, he takes out a card from his wallet and hands it to her. "Come tomorrow morning and we can chat."

The witch takes the card and pretends to read it. Pablo turns and continues down his path. He's found his model.

The house still bears the remnants of a glorious past, when Barrio 11 was an up-and-coming scene, where textile businessmen wanted to both work and live. Then the house was turned into a sweatshop. Then a fire gutted it, the owner died, and, having no heirs, it was left abandoned. A small-time gang of squatters quickly moved in. Clumsy and inexperienced, they were arrested and swiftly jailed. The ministry decided to set up Maese there, buying time to figure out a long-term solution for the house.

The commissioner, Filipuzzi, who is there to give Maese the keys, now stands at the door, visibly moody. Beside him an awkward little man with hands like spiders smiles up at him. Maese extends a hand to Filipuzzi, but he's left hanging. Filipuzzi's face is dimpled with old smallpox scars. One of his eyes looks off to the side, toward Avellaneda Street, while the other bores into Maese with an angry shine. The man with the spider hands introduces himself.

"Pleased to meet you, I'm Subinspector Laperca, the commissioner's assistant."

With overt repulsion, Maese shakes the man's tiny spider hand.

Laperca shows him a set of keys and nods toward the door. "Shall we?"

Filipuzzi lights a cigarette as Maese and Laperca walk inside. It's stuffy, empty bottles strewn everywhere—the after-effects of a party that looks to have been wild. Laperca hands him the keys and gazes outside. Maese follows his eyes. The commissioner is still standing out there smoking.

"What's going on with your boss?"

"He's in a bad mood."

"Oh yeah?"

"You know . . . he's had this house ever since they kicked out the Peruvians. And now the ministry has decided to give it to you."

"I see."

"Be careful, Filipuzzi is a dangerous guy, he's capable of doing anything to get this house back."

As if he had heard this, Filipuzzi whistles sharply and, with a nod of his head, orders Laperca to come out.

"Now you know. Be on the lookout. Bye."

Maese had met Ascanio under strange circumstances, and due to Maese's effeminate mannerisms, the young man had assumed Maese was gay, and offered him his services. Ascanio was a street kid who'd do anything to survive. The offer had flattered Maese, who liked to think of himself as attractive to this kid who was agile and slim, with the toned muscles of men whose basic formation had taken place in the open air of the streets. Maese had corrected him, and then adopted him as an assistant. Ascanio was strong and never said no to any job Maese offered. He was especially handy at moving the heavy sculptures around the studio. Every once in a while he had to rescue the boy from a police station for getting into a fight or for stealing—he always got out thanks to the bribes Maese dished to the officers. This also gave Maese power over the kid, and he believed this pacified the boy. He also hired another kid who they called Memo. Ascanio instantly gained the upper hand, and the two established a relationship in which Memo always obeyed Ascanio's orders. In resentful submission, Memo resigned himself to doing any job that repulsed Ascanio. The cast was completed with Roberta, the old maid who'd been with Maese forever.

A week later, with the ministry's advance, the studio is now in perfect order, and Maese awaits a visit from the minister. He had asked that Maese showcase his work, which Maese now has propped up, as if haphazardly, around the expansive living room, though of course he's been meticulous about making sure that each piece is set under the most favorable light. In the center stands the fountain made of polyester resin on which he'd transcribed an homage to Degas: *Woman in Her Bath, Sponging Her Legs*. The piece always makes an impact. Maese makes sure to position himself far enough away from the statue so that it won't seem too obvious that he's trying to draw attention to it, but not far enough away so that the minister misses it. The doorbell rings and Maese clears his throat, signaling Ascanio to get it.

To Maese's surprise, the minister has not come alone. An exuberant and vulgar blonde is standing next to him, overly made up and strident, with rigid, gelled hair. It is Gladys, the minister's wife. Her mouth is large, and Maese can't help but think it's a result of talking too much: she doesn't slow down, not even to breathe. As soon as she sees the fountain, she goes up to it, giving little shouts of excitement. Maese represses his impulse to stop her—he doesn't want the woman to touch it, worrying she'll stain it with her lotioned hands. Maese shows them his work and they talk amiably, the minister expressing satisfaction in having employed such an exalted artist. It's as if he's purchased Maese for his own personal use. The fact that he's so pleased calms Maese.

The door swings open, and all three turn to look. In the doorway stand the witch and her daughter, and just behind the two, Ascanio. The minister and his wife seem stricken with revulsion as they eye the ragged pair and then turn back with an interrogating look at Maese. He feels a storm of anger rise up his esophagus, though he manages to contain himself.

"Ascanio, please show the women into the kitchen, I'll be in shortly."

The assistant obeys and hurries the women out of the room. The minister and his wife stare rudely at them until the door is completely shut. There's an uncomfortable silence that, of course, Gladys interrupts.

"Ohhh, my love bug, I adore this fountain. Will you buy it for me?"

Maese cuts in before the minister can say a word: "Oh, Gladys, I'm so sorry but that would be impossible, this piece has already been sold to the US ambassador—he brought it over only so that I could package it for him to take to Houston."

Gladys pouts, and the minister puts his hands on her shoulders.

"Don't let it get to you, my little bug, I'm sure Pablo can offer you another one . . . Isn't that true, Pablo?"

"At your service."

"I know what you can do!" Gladys exclaims. "You can make something for our new flat . . . It's so empty."

"Good idea."

"On Saturday we're having a barbecue. Come on over and we'll see what you come up with."

"I'd love to."

"Maese, this is totally separate, it'll come straight from my pocket, so I hope you give us a good price."

"That won't be a problem, I'll only charge you for the materials. Does that sound okay to you?"

"You see that, my love? Maese is a true artist."

Maese happily observes Ascanio as the assistant readies the worktable. The boy has black curly hair and epitomizes the Greek ideal of masculinity. He moves around the studio with the sensuality of a cat, his eyes glowing like embers amongst ashes. He finishes setting up the pencils, one next to the other in a perfect row. He lays down the 300 gram Schoeller paper. He brushes the table to eliminate any last bit of dust and finally turns toward Maese. In front of the table he's set a red daybed where the model will lie to be sketched.

"Call the girl."

Ascanio goes out and Maese sits down at his worktable. A few moments later, Ascanio returns with the girl, Rita. The witch, her mother, follows them. Maese gives Ascanio a disdainful look, but the boy only offers a shrug as a form of apology. Rita is wearing a silk robe that Maese himself has bought her, and following his instructions, she's wearing nothing underneath. With a gesture he asks her to stand next to the daybed. Rita obeys. The witch stands beside her and peers at Maese with inquisitive eyes.

The witch doesn't move a finger. Something in her face is waiting, expectant. Maese understands that she's selling her daughter. The good thing is that he's willing to buy her. He puts his hand in his pocket, pulls out three bills, and holds them out to her. The witch's eyes light up as she takes them and stuffs them in her bra.

"Why don't you go shopping with Ascanio."

When they've both gone, Maese walks to the door, closes it, turns the key twice, returns to his desk, takes up a sharpened number 2 pencil, straightens his glasses, and finally looks at Rita.

"Please take off the robe and lie down on the couch."

What she does gives him shivers: she lets the robe slip off her as if she's been practicing this her whole life. The fabric falls like liquid down to her feet, leaving her slim, sleek body perfectly bare, exposing her subtle curves, her small flushed breasts, her discreet, promising sex. Her mouth is slightly open, her breath is short—as if she is awaiting something imminent, large—and the look on her face devilishly combines both innocence and provocation. Maese watches her lean back onto the couch as if it were in slow motion, the way people experience the slowing of time in the midst of a catastrophe, when everything seems unreal. He begins drawing her, his inspired pencil flying across the page, sketching out the sensual, tender lines of the body on the other side of the room. He couldn't have found a better, more inspiring model. Drawing her feels like he is possessing her, as if his pencil were his own sex running over her body; meanwhile, there is a stir in his pants. He draws her again and again, frantically, filling up page after page, hour after hour. The light starts to fade.

Maese finally stands, takes a lamp, and focuses it on Rita. He approaches to brush aside a few strands of hair that have fallen in front of her mouth. She looks deeply into his eyes. He can feel her breath, and it is like a chemical reaction, almost explosive. They kiss—each diving into the abyss of each other.

These are glorious days for Maese. It turns into a ritual: each afternoon Ascanio leads Rita to the studio, helps her undress, and sets her up on the couch. He then goes away, leaving them alone. When he finishes the commission for the minister and his wife, he decides he'll sculpt something with the two youths—Rita and Ascanio, each so beautiful—together. By day he draws Rita and by night he draws her sex with his own. She has returned him his youth, his enthusiasm, his will to live and create. He's started cooking again, giving himself to the sensuality of flavor, texture, aroma. The witch is happy, pulling in her daily bribe to leave Rita in Maese's hands. Ascanio hovers about, with his mischievous, almost elfin glare, which Maese reads as a sign of complicity. He finishes sketch after sketch for the Eva Perón monument, each of them better, more powerful and harmonious than the last. He still, however, has an enormous task ahead of him—he's decided to forge the sculpture with the classical method of wax smelting, following the instructions laid out by Benvenuto Cellini in *Vita*, the autobiography of the ingenious master.

The only worry Maese has these days is that someone had tried to break into his studio when nobody was there. He noticed that the back door's handle had been broken. Luckily, he never uses the back door and a dresser had been placed in front of it, so whoever tried to force it open hadn't been able to get in.

Still, to be safe, Maese takes his pistol from his house and stashes it in the studio because, as Blades says, it will unburden him of any ill. One other disturbing detail is Filipuzzi's visit to see how things were moving along, to see if he needed anything. Just an excuse to spy on him. He couldn't break his ugly gaze away from Rita. Filipuzzi unsettles Maese, especially after the warning by the spider-handed subinspector.

He is sorry when the day comes to go to the minister's barbecue. He would have preferred to continue with his routine of art and sex, but he can't snub his benefactor, and besides, he might be able to figure out a way to keep the money coming in and Rita in his studio. He considers bringing Rita along, but figures it would look bad. He decides to go with Ascanio, and have him drive. Maese hates driving.

"But Maestro," Ascanio says, "it would be a mistake to leave the house unattended. Think of all the art you have here. Living in a city of thieves, we need to be on guard day and night. Let me stay back. I'll take advantage of your absence to organize and clean up, as well as keep an eye on things."

Appetizers, grilled meats, dessert, long conversations—it drags on and on. A swarm of harrumphing public officials with sharp suits and ordinary women make up the crew at the minister's gathering. Everybody seems to stuff himself to the point of dyspepsia. Maese, however, feels a pit of anguish in his stomach that barely lets him get any food down at all. He wants to head back to his studio, to draw Rita. He realizes that the girl has become for him an almost desperate necessity.

Each minute without her is an agony that only her presence can possibly relieve. Gladys walks toward him. She, like one of the fat pachyderms in a Botero painting, is the polar opposite of Rita, who is as ethereal and smooth as Botticelli's *Venus*. Maese smiles at Gladys, who takes him by the arm.

"Come, professor. I'll show you where I want to put the sculpture you're going to make for me." She smiles, and then adds, "Make for *us*, I mean."

It's a blank white wall facing the garden, which can only be seen from the pool area. An idea for a sculpture hits him immediately, though he doesn't tell her right away. He walks around, looking at the wall from different angles, squinting his eyes. Intrigued, Gladys watches his movements. Maese acts as if he's deeply meditating on the cosmic laws that will dictate what artwork should fill that space, but in reality he's only thinking of Rita.

He approaches Gladys with an air of intrigue. "I think I know what we should do here—"

The minister calls to them from behind, interrupting the moment of intimacy: "Hey, what's this? You've gotten a little too close . . ."

"Oh, come on, love bug. Don't be stupid. The maestro was about to tell me what he's going to make for us."

"Great, then . . . illuminate us."

Maese straightens up and takes on the air of somebody about to make a grand revelation. "I'll make a fountain that will reflect the trees around the house and the pool. It will be a natural scene, a sort of conceptual congeries of the hunting trophies you have in your living room."

The minister puffs up like a bullfrog.

"I told you, love bug. Pablo is a genius. A goddamn genius. Get started as soon as you can."

"As soon as I finish the Eva monument, I'll begin."

The disappointment is visible on Gladys's face. "But that will take a long time . . ."

"Start it now, Maese," the minister says. "The monument can be done later, and testing Gladys's patience is not a pretty sight."

"As you wish."

"Come on, let's tell all the guests about the plan. They're going to die of jealousy. And a few of them will probably try to contract you as well. Just remember that when you give me the bill."

The announcement has the effect the minister expected. Several of the other guests ask Maese for his card. A few others approach him to chat. He is talking to a very short couple— they seem Lilliputian, nearly dwarfs—when something that the woman says to him, or maybe one of her gestures, sets off a rush of memories in him. Poignant memories—of Rita and Ascanio, shared looks of understanding, Ascanio's hand lingering for an extra moment on Rita's back as he helps her take off her robe, their shared laughter emanating from the hallway, Ascanio's insistence to stay behind at the studio. The mental images make him suspicious, then the suspicion turns into certainty. He feels an urgency to return to the studio. He says goodbye as quickly as he can, gets in his car, and drives like a demon all the way home, ignoring stoplights and speed limits.

Forty minutes later, the witch, watching from the window, sees Maese pull up and calls out the alarm loudly enough for Maese to hear: "Rita, Ascanio! The maestro is back!"

He finds them in the studio with their clothes ruffled and looks of fear on their faces, just getting off the couch—*his* couch! An insane fit of jealousy takes hold of him: the sacrilege, the profanity committed by these backstabbers boils his blood. He opens the top drawer of his desk and takes out a pistol, points it at Rita, then Ascanio, and then the witch. He stares at each of them, and then looks back at the boy.

"You coward, you traitor. I'm going to kill you."

Ascanio doesn't lift a finger to defend himself, but pleads and sobs for his life. Maese decides to finish him off, and then do the same with the mother and daughter, yet he falters. He'd get his revenge, but he'd probably fall into the hands of Filipuzzi, lose the favor of the minister, and also lose his freedom. Reason drowns out his fury. But what to do? He can't stand here threatening them forever. He decides to get his revenge slowly. He looks at Ascanio and, with a smile, demands, "Take off this ring of mine and give it to her," gesturing to Rita, "because you're going to marry her."

Ascanio obeys immediately. "Don't kill me. I'll do anything you say."

Maese sends Memo to hunt down a notary, and then points the gun at the mother and daughter. "A notary is coming, as well as some witnesses. I'll immediately shoot whoever utters a word." He turns back to Ascanio.

"Just promise that you won't kill me and I'll do anything you say."

Before the notary and witnesses, the terrified couple signs the nuptial contract and legally marries. As soon as the officials leave the house, Maese pulls Rita into his room by her hair, smacking and cursing her along the way. Then he rapes her, over and over, beating her all the while.

The next day he gets back to his sketches, picks up his favorite, adds a few lines, touches it up, and orders Rita to pose for him, for hours, in the most painful positions he can think of. Afterward, he punishes her with more forced sex. Days and days thus pass, as he begins to form the mold of clay that will become the fountain promised to Gladys and the minister.

The maid, Roberta, who tends to Rita's wounds after each of her beatings, approaches Maese one afternoon and glares at him.

"What?"

"You shouldn't treat that girl so cruelly."

"Roberta, don't you know how she and her mother betrayed me under my very own roof?"

"But señor, that's typical in this country. There's not a single husband that, as the saying goes, doesn't have a pair of horns on his head."

Maese covers the mold in wax and then covers the wax in clay. He fires the whole thing and pours copper alloy into the space left by the melted wax. Once it is full of bronze, he leaves it to cool, chips away the clay covering, and reveals the frieze of Rita, naked in all of her beauty, amidst a landscape of beasts, trees, and the fruit of the earth. Reclining back, the figure holds in one hand a pitcher pouring water, while her other hand is wrapped around the powerful neck of a stag, whose impressive pair of antlers has eighteen points bursting out of the frieze. The artist smiles contentedly—the sculpture is perfect down to the smallest detail. He calls Rita to his side, puts one arm around her, and pats her butt.

"Look how well your husband came out, Rita. He gave me horns once. I give him horns not every day, but for all of eternity."

YOU'VE SPOKEN MY NAME

BY ENZO MAQUEIRA

Almagro

Translated by John Washington

T
he promoter goes into the church because it's the
only place she can hide, because she thinks the priest
might be able to help her, because she'll be safe. What
she never expected was that she would walk right into a Mass.

The church, the House of Jesus, is connected to her old
school. It is Saturday. Seven thirty in the evening. Outside
it is autumn, cold, almost nobody in the streets. A memory
comes to her from when she was little and used to attend this
same church. The reminiscence only lasts a second, no more,
because it doesn't matter, nothing matters anymore. The only
thing she asks for is that the priest stop talking, that the narcos don't come into the church to kill her, that she can catch
her breath before she has a heart attack. She asks for all this
while looking up at Jesus on the altar, peering into his eyes
and clenching her fists in her pockets, squeezing the last of
her cash in her sweaty hand.

"The paths that lead to Christ are narrow, but they are
narrow precisely because they lead to Christ," the priest says,
and then, hands held out, pauses. She hates that the priest is
taking his time, but she can't do anything about it, she has to
stay unseen, she doesn't even want to raise her head, not that
she has the strength to, and the priest intones, "Salvation, the
sons of God, his sheep . . ."

She doesn't need a sermon. What she needs is another bag of cocaine, and if she doesn't get cocaine, then at least she wants to hear something to calm her down, something to convince her that she's not going to die, that the narcos aren't hiding behind the palm trees and waiting for her anymore. She's always liked the patio at the House of Jesus, ever since she started going to school in the same building and her mother walked with her the two blocks from their house. She would imagine that paradise looked just like that patio, with those big palms, those jungle plants in pots, the little birds digging after worms. But now, more than ever, she knows that paradise doesn't exist, that the drug dealers could be waiting somewhere on that patio, aiming their guns at the church door, waiting for her to come out.

"Though," the priest continues with a voice that booms off the walls and high ceilings, "the path to the devil is wide, full of colorful lights . . ." He opens his arms, palms up. "It is the path of the devil."

She starts thinking of all the mistakes she's made, one after another, her situation sinking in, deeper and deeper. The first mistake was not paying the money she owed to her dealer. She owed him so much that she couldn't even call him anymore. So she tried calling a few other people she knew, but nobody was around. It was a long weekend. She was the only one who had stayed in the city, so she was going to have to find a dealer in some other neighborhood. She decided she'd ask some of the black men. Or the Peruvians, Bolivians, the indigents who make a living day-laboring. It seemed like it would be easy, but now here she is, sitting through Mass, a cold sweat running down her back, surrounded by old women and girls her age. In the pew behind her there is a guy with a mustache, two old women, one half asleep. Any of these Bible-thumpers might work for the narcos. The narcos have their reach everywhere, as she well knows. She knows more than anybody. She grips her head, squeezes her eyes tight—she has to make it through, anyway she can, she has to make it.

It started with marijuana, then LSD; there was a period of Ecstasy. From Ecstasy to cocaine was just a single step. Was that her first mistake—starting to use coke? Because there was a time when she didn't even want to be with anybody that wasn't using. It got even worse, to the point where she never wanted to leave her room; she'd spend an entire week locked in her apartment, snorting line after line until she'd snorted all of her drugs and had spent all of her money. And when she wanted to return to work, none of the agencies, which she'd left hanging so many times, returned her calls. Her mom and dad were far away, she didn't have any girlfriends left, no guy to lend her money without having to pay him with sex first. She needed to find a new job, but first she needed to find some money to get some coke. She scoured the corners of her apartment until she came up with two hundred pesos in the bottom of a drawer. It was enough to buy another bag. It wasn't much, but it was better than nothing. She called her dealer, though she knew he wasn't going to answer; the last time they talked he'd told her that if she didn't pay he was going to run her over with his car. Which is why the promoter, dressed as inconspicuously as possible, went out to score in her neighborhood. She started at the Peruvian market, making a fool of herself: she'd never been to Peru, she told a woman working a market stand, but she'd always wanted to see Machu Picchu . . . in Peru they chew coca leaves, right? The Incans chew coca. The market woman squatted on the ground and arranged the tomatoes; she didn't even turn her head to look at the promoter. What do they eat over there? the promoter asked. I mean in Peru.

Is there good beef? But the woman said that she didn't know what they eat in Peru because "we are from Bolivia, señorita," and then she looked up into her eyes and the promoter said that she was sorry, and left, embarrassed. She was just about to head back to her apartment and deal with the comedown, but no, her second mistake: she kept looking.

The priest finally finishes the sermon, a blond girl plays a guitar and sings, the priest is moving as if in slow motion, and she can barely stand it. She looks up at the ceiling: babies with wings, an old man with a beard pointing his finger, the lights of the street coming in through the stained glass; and she's shaking again, the song of the blond girl with the voice of a transvestite ringing in her ears, the House of Jesus falling down on top of her.

She recalculated: she couldn't keep running up and down the neighborhood until she found a dealer. It was too dangerous. Better to hit up the bars in the Guardia Vieja neighborhood. The hip area of Almagro. She'd been there a few times. The bars were always filled with musicians, writers, theater people. And the inevitable mama's boy selling dope. Maybe she'd find one of the kids she used to see with her dealer. It might turn out to be an easy fix, except when she showed up she realized that it was still early and the bars weren't even open yet. She felt that cold humidity of the Buenos Aires autumn, the sidewalk carpeted with dry leaves, pigeons resting on the power lines cutting apart the sky above her. She felt like she was the last person in the world. She looked through the windows of the apartments she was passing and imagined the couples cuddling inside, under warm covers, caressing each other's feet. But not her. She was alone. But even in this she was wrong. She wasn't the only one in the street; on the opposite corner she spotted an old beggar woman, who was always asking for *monedas* from passersby. *Monedita*, the promoter had nicknamed her, though she had never actually spoken to her. Whenever Monedita approached to ask for her change she would walk faster, scared that the old woman was going to rob her. She did the same thing this time: she crossed the street away from Monedita, just as three Peruvians stepped out of an old house she was passing.

The priest is smiling now, the old women in front of her bow their heads, the wood of the pews creaks. *How much longer is Mass?* she asks herself. She can't stand it any longer, her comedown making her feel like she is falling, uncontrollably spinning.

She should have given up when those black men looked her up and down after she approached them.

"The young woman thinks we have drugs, does she? Just because we're Peruvian?" one of them sneered.

She shook her head no, even waved her hand, and then held up a finger: not at all, she swore, she just asked because they seemed like they might know where she could get some.

"And why did it seem like we might know?" the man had asked her. "Next time, just give us a kiss." He approached her and tried to smack her on the ass, but she ran, one block, two, until she couldn't run any farther and she bent over, put her hands on her knees, sucking in air on the corner of Corrientes and Medrano. Traffic was a mess. A truck had run into a taxi and the cops had blocked off half the road. The promoter had crossed Corrientes, weaving between the buses, through the blasting car stereos, the motorcycles cutting in and out of lanes. There were so many people. It had been too early to score. She was about to give up, ready to spend the rest of her

Saturday sinking into a comedown when she felt something tug on her arm. It was Monedita. She was breathing heavily, looking up at her from her creased eyes. Her reaction was automatic. She reached down into her pocket to see if she'd been robbed.

"Relax, mami," Monedita had said. "What are you looking for? A little pigeon shit?"

The promoter didn't understand.

"A little pigeon shit," Monedita repeated, and then tapped the side of her nose with a finger. "Do you want a little pigeon shit or don't you?"

She hadn't expected Monedita to have what she wanted. She was too desperate, and couldn't afford that luxury. She followed her toward the train tracks, to the bridges and the squats on the south side. In one of the shacks lining the edge of the cliff above the tracks, Monedita knocked on a couple doors, but nobody opened. She knocked again and a woman pointed her to another house.

"We're almost there. Are you going to make it?" Monedita asked, peering at the promoter, who had felt as if her legs were going to give out—everything was spinning and it seemed like the spinning would never stop. Somehow, she was able to walk all the way to Rivadavia. Monedita rang the bell of an old house whose door was covered in graffiti. The promoter didn't think anybody would answer. Another mistake: not to take off running right then, go to a hospital to get a shot to end her suffering. Instead, she'd stuck with Monedita, following her down a dark hallway, climbing a set of stairs. A few doors opened as they passed: Peruvians, Bolivians, homeless, looking at her and then slamming their doors shut, pushing out wafts of fried food. Monedita climbed the stairs, complaining about her knees, saying that they were almost there as she stopped to rest. They had climbed up to the third floor. A spoiled mama's boy, bearded, not more than thirty years old, was waiting for them next to his open door. Monedita walked into the apartment, whispering something to him as she passed. The mama's boy wore a Rolex on his left wrist. Though he seemed like trouble, the promoter had felt a tenderness toward him. Her fifth mistake. Or maybe sixth. She couldn't keep track of them anymore.

"We pray that this sacrifice, which is mine and yours, be accepted by Our Father the All Powerful," the priest says with the host held high. She's uncomfortable in the pew, not knowing where to put her hands, occasionally placing a palm on her chest to slow down her heart. For a moment it seems to stop beating, and then the next moment it is beating too fast. She squeezes her chest with her hot hand. She doesn't want to die in the company of these old women, the old man with the look of pity, the girls her age who have probably never even smoked a joint. They pray, all of them, and though she remembers how to pray, she can't bring herself to do it.

"So you're looking for some coke?" the mama's boy had said, leaning forward and down into the face of the promoter, who had taken a seat in the room's only chair, with Monedita standing in the corner biting her nails. "Okay, little lady," the man said, staring into her eyes, "I have good news for you."

Who is this idiot? She knew skinny guys like him, but he was especially ridiculous. Her quick dismissal of him had been yet another mistake. The promoter explained that she barely had any money, that she could get more soon, but right now she was desperate, and she stopped to think, and then continued: so desperate that she was willing to do anything to get a little coke. She meant it too. She was trembling in fear, but she was serious: *anything*, she had said, but also regretting it as soon as the man smiled at her, nodding his head slowly, still nodding, and then checking the time on his Rolex and taking out his phone to make a call.

"Get it ready," he said to someone on the other end of the line. "I found someone for the job."

When he got off the phone he turned back to the promoter, looking into her eyes, getting close enough so that she could smell the alcohol on him. The bad boy told her it was her lucky day, that he was going to give her a lot of coke, just as long as she did him a favor.

"How much coke?" she asked him.

How much coke? the guitar repeats over and over, the blonde singing another eardrum-shattering song, a line of Bible-thumpers filling out the central aisle, the old ladies up front, then the girls her age, and then guy in the back who walks past the promoter, gives her a look, licks his lips, and then enters into the communion line.

"A brick," the bad boy had said to her.

A brick. A kilo of cocaine. The man took a baggy out of his pocket, dipped his fingernail inside, and offered a bump to the promoter. She sucked in as deeply as she could. She felt the cocaine pass through her nose, tingle her mouth, and then shoot into her veins. Now, yes, she was ready to do whatever it took. She'd told him twice, so that he would believe her, but now the bad boy wouldn't even look at her. He'd grabbed his phone again, was making another call, telling someone to send "that dude" to the Medrano station. He hung up and then made another call, asking for two men to go along with "the young lady" to Medrano.

"And you're going to stay here," he told Monedita, putting

his phone back in his pocket. The promoter hardly believed what was happening. A kilo of coke. Nothing else mattered. The guy told her they would explain to her what she needed to do once she got to the station. "My boys," he said, "my boys will take care of everything."

She was instructed to meet a man underneath the second ventilator located on the downtown track in the Medrano subway station. That was it. The boy promised her that when she came back to the apartment the brick would be waiting for her.

"We know where you live," he told her, and he pointed at her with his finger, showing off a fat silver ring with two initials on it that she couldn't make out. He got up close to her again, even closer than before. "Do I need to tell you what will happen to you if you don't do what we tell you?"

The promoter looked him straight in the eyes: the guy was starting to scare her. Two black men approached out of nowhere and stood on either side of the door. They were both short, with sharp jaws. It was only in this moment that the promoter started to realize how much danger she was in. She started shaking, in part because the coke was reaching her brain, but also because she knew that she was so close to scoring. "Take it easy," Monedita said. "They'll take care of you." And then one of the black men closed the door.

You came to the shore,
Searching for neither the rich nor the wise.
Desiring only that I follow You.
Lord, You have looked into my eyes,
Smiling, and speaking my name.
I have left my boat on the shore,
And together with You, I will seek another sea.

* * *

The priest walks slowly back to the altar, his bald and pinkish head bowed down. Her heart is beating too fast again, as if it were about to burst and kill her in the middle of the service, which she hopes doesn't happen. She doesn't want to die in front of these old women. She closes her eyes. The Mass seems like it's about to be over, and she'll be able to talk with the priest—*Just one word from you is enough to heal me*—like that prayer she used to recite as a child, but no, it's not over yet, the priest says that he forgot to do the collection, and he laughs. "With age one tends to forget," he says, and then he points to two women on the end of an aisle who take up a black velvet bag and walk along the pews collecting donations. The priest raises his arms and explains what they'll use the money for: our needy brothers from the north, the program to help kids addicted to drugs. The old women lean toward the velvet bag and release bills from their claw-like hands. A man in a suit, little boys. Another man. When the ladies with the collection bag approach the promoter, she puts her head down and a drop of sweat falls to the marble floor.

But what if they kill her after she does her part of the job? She was walking toward Medrano, the two black men directly behind her. They were only a couple of blocks away. She couldn't trust a drug dealer. She thought about escaping, turning onto Perón, but the men were following too closely. It would be too dangerous. And maybe they were telling the truth—a kilo of coke, a white brick, and the entrance to the metro closer with every step.

When she got down the stairs one of the men grabbed her by the arm and stopped her. "See that guy there?" he said. "See him? That's the one you're going to push onto the tracks."

The guy had his back turned to them, he was standing under the second air vent, close to the edge of the tracks. Another man next to him seemed to have brought him there.

"I'm not going to push anybody," the promoter heard herself say, her voice barely escaping her body.

"Wait until the train comes and then just shove him," the man instructed.

Again, she refused. No. No way. And yet she couldn't brush away the image of a brick of cocaine, and her hands took the metro card that the other man handed her; they walked her to the turnstile and somehow, unable to resist them, she stayed on her feet and passed through to the platform. The two men stayed on the other side of the gates, watching her and talking. She didn't have any options. She couldn't escape. They were about to give her enough coke to last a year. The promoter slowly approached the man. The guy she was supposed to push was standing there, close to the rails, his back turned. The man next to him glanced toward the promoter, nervous, seemingly ready to take off running. The promoter started shaking when the lights of the next train appeared, like a mirage at the end of the tunnel. It was so easy. She couldn't fail. But if she did, would that bad boy kill her? Even if she did what they asked, they could still kill her. *These kinds of people,* she thought to herself, *are capable of anything.* She was thinking too much—another mistake—and then the train broke out of the tunnel so fast she didn't have time to react; it pulled into the station, braking, coming to a stop, and opened its doors. The guy entered and was lost in the crowd of the subway car.

The last rays of the sunset were falling when the promoter recognized the church's cupola above the other buildings.

The oldest church in Almagro, the same stained glass she'd looked up to as a child, the smell of incense, the old women dressed in furs. She was able to get away from the two men because they weren't expecting her to run as fast as she ran, dashing through the emergency exit, scrambling up the stairs two at a time. It also helped that it was starting to get dark outside and there were more people in the street, people going to the movies, or the theater, or some other place where she wouldn't be able to go. She couldn't even return to her apartment. She needed to find somewhere safe, someone to help her, the priest, to drag her out of this hell.

The parting blessing: "Go in peace," the priest says. The blond girl starts the last song and the man behind her, the kids, the old men and women, start streaming out of the church, slowly, too slowly, the minutes seeming like an eternity. Nobody looks at her, though it seems like everybody is staring, the humid air of the streets sweeping in, not much time left; she turns to look outside: it's night already, and she can't see anybody hiding behind the palms. She tries to breathe in some of the outside air as the priest closes the door, there's nobody but the two of them now, she just needs a minute to clear her head, gather strength, stop the buzzing in her ears, walk the Stations of the Cross up to the sacristy. She manages to stand, pulling herself up with the back of the pew. She walks as well as she can. She knocks on the sacristy door with her white knuckles. The priest opens without asking who it is, and tells her that if she wants to confess she'll have to wait a bit. The promoter doesn't know how to begin. She is at a loss for words.

"It's pretty bad, huh? Whatever mess sent you my way," the priest says. He has his glasses on, the top button of his collar still tight. She doesn't respond, she can't, can't even try.

It's as if what she wanted to explain isn't real. Not as real as the bills of ten, twenty, fifty pesos sticking out of the velvet bag behind the priest. Or as real as the iron cross, the bottom end sharpened like a stake, hanging from the wall. Her last effort: a quick motion that takes the priest by surprise. With all that money she could pay her dealer. She would even have enough money to buy more. *How much more?* she wonders. A bag, maybe two, a couple days more of sniffing coke. And then, later, she'll figure out what's next.

Now she's going to commit her last mistake. Now she's going to kill a man.

THREE ROOMS AND A PATIO

BY ELSA OSORIO

Núñez

Translated by John Washington

Núñez, three large rooms with a patio/garden. And within her parents' budget, slightly higher, but they can counteroffer. Núñez is far, her boyfriend told her. An hour by bus from downtown.

"It's not that far. Don't exaggerate."

Her parents wouldn't be going downtown every day anyway, as they'd be retired by the time they moved into the apartment. And as for Norma, who would live there for the year, she wouldn't mind the commute.

Plus, she likes the idea of living in a more peaceful setting, with trees and even a patio! What a luxury. And she doesn't even know where she'll be assigned to teach anyway; today she is heading to Caballito, but tomorrow she could be sent somewhere else, she goes wherever she's needed. So she decides to check out this apartment, as well as some others, since the specific neighborhood isn't the most important thing to her. It is just one of many things to keep in mind, including light and street noise.

For Norma, Núñez is a warm place smelling of jasmine. And Silvio, her old chemistry teacher—*papers strewn on the floor of his office, his hands on her body, the kisses, how lovely you are, newborn desires, one and then another afternoon. Today you will teach me physics; of course, my girl, just for a few minutes,*

because that afternoon, before Silvio's mother returned, she let,
for the first time, her desires grow, the moistness between her legs,
opening everything for him, not even knowing what was happening
because she should have run and the next day at three they were
in bed again, savoring each other, laughing, playing games, sniffing
out desire . . .

Silvio taught her chemistry and physics, and Norma
passed her final exams, the last hurdle to her bachelor's degree. Afterward, she moved to Rosario, where her parents had
been for the last three years. She and Silvio parted ways with
plans to write, to see each other again, but then time passed,
further studies, new people, a different city.

When they ran into each other years later in Buenos
Aires, Silvio laughed when Norma told him that she was in
her third year studying physics and chemistry, and he made
a slightly off-color joke, eluding to their previous meetings,
but she thought it was funny. So much so that they slept together again that day, though Norma was already dating Luis.
Silvio, so different, so apart from the seductive engineering
student who had been her teacher, and not because he was
working as an engineer, not because his mother had died and
he now supported himself, but because his way of looking at
the world had matured; he explained what was happening in
society with the same enthusiasm he'd had when teaching
physics, yet with more passion. Norma listened to him with
the same affection and admiration she had for him before,
but she didn't really listen; even though he was right, she preferred not to get involved in politics. Norma wasn't going to
solve the world's problems; nor was Silvio.

They saw each other three or four more times, when she
was in Buenos Aires for a seminar, or simply to spend a day
there, and she found him increasingly serious, with less free

time. At one of their rendezvous, they discussed the fact that Silvio didn't like how Norma still acted like a child.

"Wake up, Norma," he said. "Wake up and do something with your life." And then, bothered, he told her that they couldn't go back to his house, that he needed to work. He told her to go and window-shop, that he was busy with what was going on in the world. Norma was worried about leaving him like that, after a fight, although her life really had nothing to do with his anymore, and who knew when she'd be back in Buenos Aires. They finally said goodbye with a hug, and then a kiss, and just as she was about to hail a cab, she said: "God, I still want you." And the day opened up, hours extended by skin, hands, bodies, sweat, with joy, with desperation, as if they knew this would be the last time.

The next morning he told her that he couldn't accompany her to the bus station—he had an appointment—and that was when she happened to see his gun, and asked him, "Are you crazy, Silvio?"

"No, I know what I'm doing."

"Be careful, please."

"You too," and he gave her a kiss on the forehead, and then said again, "Wake up, Norma," followed by another kiss, this time on her lips.

She could never find him again; he never answered his phone or the letters she sent him. She thought that maybe he'd left the country after the military took over, but he could have at least written to say goodbye! The only friend they had in common was Natalia, and she hadn't heard anything from Silvio either.

"It's odd," Norma said to her, "I haven't seen him in a year now; he's not at home and he doesn't answer my letters."

His older sister, whose number Natalia found in a telephone book, answered drily when they called, saying that he went on a trip and she didn't know where.

"Another exile," Norma conjectured—she had lots of friends who'd left the country in those years, since '75; and others, even worse, those who were . . . taken, no one knowing anything more.

Norma hops out of the 8 bus and walks down Jaramillo Street; Silvio's smiling face comes back to her, that intense stare of his, that last time they saw each other: *Wake up, Norma; do something with your life.*

The property is on the corner of Zapiola and Jaramillo, just a few blocks from Silvio's old house. The young woman showing the place, Ana, is nice, and also pretty. When they are about to leave the real estate office a man walks in, tough looking, and he begins speaking to Ana. He glances at Norma for a moment, seemingly annoyed at her presence, his steely eyes boring into her.

"I'll wait for you out front," Norma tells Ana. "Don't be too long."

Once they are both back out on the street, Ana reiterates how peaceful the neighborhood is, and Norma agrees, saying she knows the area.

"Ah, so you're from around here?"

"No, I'm from Rosario, but I lived in Buenos Aires, and I had some friends who lived in this neighborhood, though I don't remember where exactly."

Maybe she lies because they are just turning onto Vidal, and Norma is hoping that Ana doesn't notice how odd she's feeling when, step by step, they approach the very building Silvio lived in. Her heart races as Ana stops in front of the door and pulls out a giant key ring, racing even faster as they enter and turn to the left, yes, right there, Silvio's place, where Norma, for the first time . . .

The door opens and Ana starts talking: "It's a little messy, but just imagine it furnished, with plants and the patio scrubbed clean." The patio that no longer smells of jasmine, and any plant life is withered and dry: maybe they didn't even bother to pull up the dead vine creeping up the railing, or plant any new flowers. The main room is empty, save for a small broken coffee table, a few ragged rugs on the floor, a shattered jar, and two ripped pillows obscenely exposing their fluffy insides. The owner is a young man who's almost never around, Ana tells her.

"Is he out of the country?" Norma asks, and there's a gleam of alert in Ana's eyes.

"No, why?"

"Oh, just because you said the owner wasn't around, so I thought that he might be out of the country. Is there nothing here but this little table? I guess you sell these places unfurnished? I don't have much experience with this." Norma forces a laugh. "I've never bought an apartment before."

"Some come furnished, and we can also sell you furniture if you need it."

They move on to the bedroom. "This room does have a large bed and two nightstands," says Ana.

That bed! A sudden sharp feeling overtakes Norma. *How beautiful you are,* she remembers Silvio whispering to her. *And you, tough boy,* she responded.

Silvio, she thinks, *where are you?*

"Something wrong?" Ana asks, interrupting her reverie.

"No, I was just wondering if my parents would like the bed or not."

"Of course they will. It's not modern or anything, and it

has that big headboard. It's classic, noble even, like they used to make them. They'll probably like it more than you. If you want it, I'll find out what the owner's asking for it."

They move into the next room, and Norma knows she must stop staring at the bed or Ana will realize something is up. The other room: papers and books strewn about, a whole mess in the middle of the floor.

The kitchen, like the bathroom, is a bit of a wreck as well. The sight of the dry plants sends shivers up Norma's spine.

"The owner never waters his plants?" she finds herself asking.

Ana, smiling, responds: "I know, he's not into plants, right? Do you want to see another apartment or go back to the office?"

"I've seen enough."

She walks with Ana to the office, tells her she's interested in that last apartment, though the price is high. Maybe it could be an investment.

She thinks about buying it right away, just as it is, but where is Silvio? *You must know,* she thinks, *you witch,* but then instead, aloud, asks Ana, "Are the papers all in order? I ask because if the owner is so absentminded . . ."

"No, everything is all set. If you're interested, I'd make an offer, because there are a few other potential buyers."

"Well, since we're both here right now, let's make sure the paperwork is all ready—the deed and all that. I don't want to make my parents come out here for nothing."

The coworker in the office, the same steely-eyed man she saw earlier, stares at her impatiently as she asks, "What is the square footage again? And do you have the layout? Are you positive the utilities are not included?"

The man calls out to Ana before she can reply to Norma.

They speak to each other quietly, and then Ana turns back toward Norma, a big smile on her face.

"Sorry, what did you want to know?"

"What's the square footage? It hasn't been foreclosed on or anything, right?"

"What about getting into these details after you make an offer?"

"Well, like I said, this is for my parents, and they're going to want these details. They're not going to make an offer without knowing the specs, and I don't want to get their hopes up if the paperwork's not squared away."

"It's squared away, miss," the man cuts in. "All of our properties are verified before they go on the market."

Norma extends her hand to the man and says, "Nice to meet you, but it seems strange to me that you don't want to give me this information when I'm an interested buyer. You're either too busy or you don't actually want to sell."

She wishes she could ask them who the real owner is, but she can't bring herself to get the question out under the man's furious gaze. *Get out of here*, she tells herself. *Just go.*

The man spits back at her: "It's not like that at all, miss. It's just that we're in the middle of a big closing right now and, well . . . Okay, Ana, give the young lady all the info she wants."

She wants to ask questions until the man explodes, but is afraid of annoying him even more. *How does this guy control Silvio's apartment?* she asks herself. *And what happened to Silvio?*

Ana gets up and speaks quietly to the repugnant man. He slams his fist down on the desk.

"You want to know if you can get the deed *right now*? What, do you have all that money in your wallet?"

Ana intervenes, smiling: "Think it over. Make an offer,

and if it's accepted, I'm sure we can arrange a quick transfer with the owner." She widens her eyes, signaling to Norma to stop bothering her boss. As if to say, *It's time to go, before the jerk behind the desk causes more problems.*

As Norma walks out the door, she shoots back one last nervous question: "Does the apartment have a phone?"

"Yeah."

A phone that hasn't been answered in months. If Silvio actually left the country, he would have left behind some paperwork for the apartment to be sold. His sister must be part owner; Norma tries to recall something Silvio once said to her, a vague memory, yes, that he didn't get along with his sister.

"I'll be in touch," Norma says to Ana.

Wake up, Norma, Silvio told her.

Should she file a complaint? But to whom? If Silvio did go abroad, what exactly would her complaint be?

If the real estate people went through everything in Silvio's apartment, they must have seen Norma's letters, and read them. Luckily, she'd given a different name at the office. Norma Bersalino, trying out what her boyfriend's name will sound like after they're married.

She goes back to Núñez, wishing that walking the streets would somehow lead her to Silvio. In Cabildo she finally finds a call center and asks for a phone book. She squeezes into a booth so that nobody can hear her. She looks up a private eye and asks for an appointment. It's urgent. Yes, she can be there in an hour.

A modest detective's office on Viamonte Street. She wants to find Silvio's old friends. From way back. She asks the detective to check if he went abroad . . . legally. "I mean," she says, "with papers." But besides his birthday, Norma doesn't know any other personal details.

"It's fine, we'll figure it out."

"I can't afford much."

"No problem, you can pay in installments. Six payments. Come back Thursday, sometime in the afternoon. It'll be hard to find his friends, but I'll try."

A kid opens the door at Silvio's sister's house and lets her in. She asks for the sister just as she and her husband walk in.

"Who is this?" the husband asks.

"A friend. She was one of Silvio's students. Back in school."

The man smiles sarcastically, making a gesture to his wife that Norma doesn't understand.

"Come on in," she says to Norma, though she's already inside. The husband hovers, keeping a close eye on Norma. But the sister doesn't know anything, surely Silvio has told her nothing.

But then, whispering, the sister says: "He was involved with something. That's all I know. And then he was gone."

"And have you filed for habeas corpus?" Norma asks, also whispering.

"No. My husband doesn't want to get involved. Doesn't want any problems. We didn't see him much anyway," she says. "And we have kids around."

"Is the apartment on Vidal his as well? Your mother bought it, right? And then put it in Silvio's name?"

The woman questions why she's asking so much about the apartment.

"I don't know. I'm worried. I want to find Silvio, and it occurs to me that he might have stopped by that apartment.

Do you know anyone, any of his friends, somebody who could help me?"

As the sister shakes her head, her husband replies, "We didn't like his friends."

Norma thanks them for their time and then, to cut the tension, asks which bus she should take to get to Cabildo and Pedraza, the 168 or the 52?

She walks back by the apartment. If anybody from the agency sees her, they'll suppose that she actually wants to buy it.

She's waiting at the taxi stand when Silvio's nephew rushes up to her. "You were asking about Silvio, right?"

"Yeah."

He hands her a paper with a name—*Beto*—and a number on it.

"It's my uncle, Silvio's cousin. They still see each other. And this is a friend of his who helped me out on a test once." He scribbles another number. "Plus Aunt Maru. She gets along with Silvio. Good luck, lady. If you find anything, call me. My name's Mauro."

She wants to hug him, but he dashes away.

She needs an accomplice; she can't do it all alone. She can't tell her boyfriend since he wouldn't understand about Silvio, especially if she told him that he was the first man she'd ever slept with. What about Gaby? Ever since returning to Buenos Aires, Norma's wanted to go see her. Gaby is married and living in Núñez.

As soon as she gets out of the taxi, she looks for a pay phone and calls Gaby, who immediately invites Norma over. *Perfect*, she thinks.

Gaby even has some news for her: she's pregnant, very

happy, yes, but also dying of fear, it's no time to be having a child, she would like to flee.

"But why?" Norma asks her. "Gaby, you're so—"

"Ay, Norma. Do you live in Rosario or on Mars?"

Norma replies that she lives in Buenos Aires now, in a hotel, until she can find an apartment to buy for her parents.

Gaby remembers some of the details Norma used to tell her about Silvio. But unfortunately, she doesn't remember where Silvio used to go for his secret meetings. Gaby drives a tiny little Fiat, given to her by her in-laws, and in it they swing by the apartment, and then park, secretively, across from the real estate office.

"It looks like it's about to close," Gaby says. "Duck down."

Ana comes out and closes the door behind her. She walks to the corner, hails a cab, and Norma and Gaby immediately start tailing her—just like in the movies, though it's easier because the taxi doesn't know it's being followed. The cab pulls over at 4300 11 de Septiembre Street, at the corner of Libertador, and Ana gets out and walks down Correa Avenue. Norma and Gaby stay on 11 de Septiembre, making sure that they're not seen, and then double back and stop at the corner of Libertador.

"There she is," Gaby says. "She's crossed the street. But where is she going? It's not possible . . ." They speed past as Ana enters the Naval School of Mechanical Engineering.

"Slow down!" Norma barks. "You're going to kill us."

"Did you see where she went? Into the ESMA! The girl is a marine! Do you know what goes on in there?"

"No."

"They torture people. Kill them. You better be careful, Norma. This could be really dangerous."

But instead of stepping back, Norma decides that she

won't give up until she finds Silvio, even if it's dangerous. To-day, she realizes, will mark a *before* and an *after* in her life.

They return to Gaby's place and call Luis; he's out with some friends, but agrees to meet up with them the following day.

Now to call those numbers that the nephew gave Norma—good kid, not like his parents. Beto doesn't answer and doesn't have a machine.

His Aunt Maru doesn't know anything either, and also sounds worried. "Are you a friend of Silvio's? Why don't you come and see me tomorrow?"

"Do you know Beto?"

"Yeah, he's Mirta's son, Silvio's cousin."

"Could you send him a message from me? That Norma called?" She gives her Gaby's number.

Not an hour passes before Beto calls from a pay phone.

"I'm Norma, Silvio's friend."

"His student?"

She feels proud that Silvio had mentioned her to some-body. "Can you talk? It's urgent."

"About what?"

She tells him that she knows something about Silvio, and wants to see if he can tell her anything else. She thinks of giving him Gaby's address, but decides instead to meet him at a pizza joint close to Silvio's old place.

She calls the private eye again. They set up a meeting for the next day, Thursday, at eleven.

"You can't meet sooner?" Norma asks.

"It's been more than a year since you've heard anything of your friend, and now you can't wait a few hours? No, I can't meet earlier."

"Please."

He gives in and tells her that Silvio didn't leave the country, and that he has a name to give her.

They start planning that night. It's the four of them now, including Leandro, Gaby's husband, and Beto, who takes charge.

The following day Norma will go to the real estate office. She'll tell them that she wants to see the apartment again, that her parents are interested. She'll take a camera and snap pictures for evidence. Her parents will have to come to see the place eventually, though Norma doesn't want to get them involved in the whole mess. They decide to pass off another couple as her parents, though they'll have to hunt down some willing partners to pull this off. After the visit, Norma will confirm her interest, make a high offer, and ask for all of the relevant paperwork.

Leandro offers to ask a friend who is almost done training to be a notary to help them with the paperwork.

"But don't we need to make an offer first?" Norma asks.

"If you have the cash," Beto tells her, "you can go straight to a notary to handle the paperwork."

"And do *you* have the cash?"

"We'll have it. Listen, Norma, this is going to work, believe me. You'll have the money and you'll act the part. We just need to get that money in order."

"And then?" Norma presses, hoping they don't see that her legs have begun to tremble, that she can't swallow. Nobody says anything. It's scary. It was Norma who called this meeting, who put the group together. *Wake up, Norma*, Silvio had said. She knows Gaby, her husband seems like a decent guy, but she's still not sure about Beto. He must be able to feel her anxiety. He cuts the meeting short.

"That's enough for today. We're tired. We each have our

work cut out for us. We'll figure out the rest tomorrow."

"Will we find Silvio?" Norma asks, her voice quivering.

Beto grabs her hand. "I don't know, Normita. But we'll either find him or avenge him."

"Avenge him?" She wants to get out of there before they realize what she's feeling and before they say what they might do. She's not going to kill anybody, not the guy at the real estate office, despite how awful he seems, and not the girl. Nobody.

Wake up, Norma.

"Tomorrow I'll talk to the detective," she says, to cover up her nerves, to be part of the group. "Though he already told me that Silvio hasn't left the country."

"Yeah, he might be involved himself. Don't even think about giving him my name," says Beto.

"Or ours," Gaby chimes in.

The name the detective has for Norma is Beto's. She remembers Beto's warning not to give too much away, and doesn't say anything. But maybe it will be fine—the detective decides not to charge her anything.

"Take care of yourself, girl," he tells her. "You should probably forget about your friend Silvio. Maybe, with some luck, they'll release him."

She thinks about suggesting that he look into a certain real estate firm in Núñez. Suddenly, however, she feels a chill climbing up her spine, and she decides to tell him nothing.

At nine the next night the same group meets back up at Gaby's along with the soon-to-be notary. Beto has new information.

They'd all done their work with a discipline that was surprising for such a new group. Norma relays her conversation with the detective; Beto tells them he filed a habeas corpus petition, and that he found out that Silvio let a friend named Colorado spend a week in the apartment. Norma shares that the girl from the firm wouldn't let her take any photos of the apartment, saying that it was too messy, and that they hadn't had time to clean up since it had just gone on the market. Norma had asked her if they could write up a contract since her parents were ready to buy.

"Without even seeing it?" Ana had replied.

"Of course they're going to see it first," Norma said. "They trust me, but not *that* much."

The almost-notary tells Norma that she should get a photocopy of the deed. Once they have that, he can look into what's going on; he assumes they will probably want to switch ownership over from Silvio to one of their own henchmen.

The only problem now is that they still need to find two people to stand in as Norma's parents. Maybe Silvio's aunt and a friend of hers? She did say she was up for anything. Beto says no—Silvio's aunt filed the habeas, and one of her family members has already gone missing. It's a bad idea.

For a moment Norma considers passing off her future in-laws as her parents. They'd be perfect. They don't know a thing, and so they'd ask questions and make comments that would seem believable. She's sure they would agree to do it, but she'd also feel guilty dragging Luis into this.

As soon as she pitches the idea to the group, they all say no. No outsiders. "Got that? Just us."

"The parents aren't necessary," Leandro says. "They can just trust their daughter on this. They'll give her the power of attorney and we'll have one less problem."

"Falsified power of attorney?"

"Of course. One false document for the notary to draw up."

The plan seems as simple and natural as buying a pair

of shoes. What none of them say, however, and what Norma doesn't even ask, is what the final objective is. When the details are put in order, when the pieces all line up with each other, then what?

They agree to meet again—after finishing their individual tasks—in two days.

Luis thinks it odd that Norma doesn't want him to come along when she meets up with her group. "If your friend is married, why don't all of us go out together?" he asks.

Frustrated, Norma tells him that she is helping Gaby with something, something important and private that she can't talk to him about.

"Just be careful," he tells her. "If she's in trouble, don't get involved. How well do you even know her?"

She nearly tells him off, but what she does instead is give him a kiss, before sweetly saying goodbye.

Norma explains her issues with the bathroom and the kitchen to Ana. She's trying to get the price down. She doesn't want any of the furniture, but she does like the bed.

But what is Ana thinking? Is she believing any of it?

After another walk-through Norma makes an offer, which, three days later, is accepted.

"In about two weeks we can sign the paperwork," the almost-notary says to Norma. "If that sounds good to everyone, I will get started on the paperwork and write up the contract. Or, rather, I'll tell Ana that I'll just hand it to my client, as I'm heading off on vacation in a few days, and then she can give it to one of my assistants."

Beto is a bit skeptical of the almost-notary since he's not an official notary yet. But Norma isn't.

"What does it matter," she asks, "if we're not actually going through with the contract?"

"Yeah, you're right," agrees Beto.

Norma then hands over the documents the firm gave her and they notice that there is a piece missing—the firm didn't include a signature. Maybe they are still deciding who will sign.

They talk through the whole plan: what Norma has to do, how many of the bad guys will be around.

"The *bad guys*, yes, they're awful," Beto says.

Norma is worried. *How did it come to this, to this ghost firm, to friends going missing?*

"You're just nervous," Gaby says, trying to calm her. "We're all here to help you."

"Normita," Beto adds, "if you're scared you don't have to stay the whole time. Just at the beginning, just to drop off the papers."

"They're not even going to read the contract. When the head guy comes in we'll have them all inside where we want them."

"And then what do I do?" Norma asks, when what she really wants to know is what *they* are going to do.

"Once it starts, just go into the bathroom, and don't come out until it's all over."

They laugh. But it's also a serious question: *What will they do?*

"We'll take them hostage," Beto says, "and then demand that they release our friend."

Norma exhales, relieved. She looks at them and smiles. All this time worrying, thinking of bloodshed, when all they want is to take them hostage. It feels good, better. And now it's time for action.

* * *

The day arrives. As planned, Norma goes to the notary office at three in the afternoon. There are two other people in the waiting room, sitting on comfortable black leather sofas. If it weren't for Gaby, who is posing as the receptionist, she would think she's in a real notary's office, and that she is there to sign a contract to buy a three-room apartment with a patio in Núñez.

"Miss Bersalino, please follow me," Gaby says.

She follows Gaby into a large room with an oval table and chairs. There is a door at the other side of the room.

"I'll take your documents, please," Gaby says. "And the power of attorney from your parents."

Beto is a genius. It all seems so legit: there are strangers in the waiting room, Gaby as the receptionist to calm Norma's nerves, even a ringing phone.

"Would you like a coffee? The notary will be with you momentarily. We're waiting for the other party to arrive."

"Just a glass of water, please," Norma says.

She never thought Beto would actually be able to pull off something like this. But where is he right now? Gaby reappears, flashes her perfect smile. "Please follow me," she says. Three men come in after her. The awful man from the real estate office, a fat man, and an incredibly skinny, hunchbacked guy who stares at the floor. All three are wearing suits.

"Have a seat. The notary is finishing up a meeting and will be with you shortly. Would you like anything to drink?"

"A coffee," the fat man says.

"Coke," the awful man says.

"And you?" Gaby asks the skinny one.

The man lifts his head slightly. His hair is greased back, and he has enormous bags under his eyes. It's Silvio! Fifteen years older and forty pounds thinner.

"A tea, please."

And then he glances at Norma. An intense but fleeting glance. Or maybe she just imagines this.

"Miss," the fat man says, "tell the notary that we don't have much time."

"And which of you is Señor Cilmes?" Gaby asks. "Your papers, please."

With a blank look on his face, Silvio hands over the documents. Norma still isn't sure if he's noticed her or not. She doesn't want him to know she's there: she's scared of what could happen, and yet, at the same time, she feels a certain pride, and wants him to see her. *Look at me. You asked me to wake up. Well, here I am.*

The almost-notary walks into the room. He seems almost as nervous as Norma. He must be thinking that the plan is thrown off with Silvio in the room. "This is Mr. Silvio Cilmes," he says. "And you two gentlemen?"

"I'm Kukier, his attorney."

"And I'm Morero, the owner of the real estate company."

"Well, this is everyone then."

The almost-notary just needs to go through a few more steps, and yet, suddenly, he shoots a frightened look at the door. Now is the moment for Norma to go to the bathroom and not come out until everything is over. But with Silvio there, poor Silvio, how can she leave?

The door opens and three men come up behind Silvio and his companions. They are carrying guns.

The almost-notary pulls out his own pistol, his hand trembling.

The man behind Silvio yells at him, "Drop your weapon or you're dead!"

Norma yells, "Not him!" just as she hears a gunshot. Her

fear doesn't stop her from running to Silvio and grabbing his arm.

The two of them rush out of the room. There is shouting, another gunshot, a door slams.

"Norma!" Silvio gasps, but she doesn't stop dragging him along.

They pass through the kitchen and approach another door.

"Are you hurt?" she asks.

"Just grazed."

"Then let's get out of here."

Outside the building they see Beto. "Good job, Normita. Jump in the blue car," he says.

"Where are you taking us?"

"To a little joint, just until this mess gets cleaned up," Beto says, winking.

It's a little place in Núñez. Not three rooms with a patio, but it will work. Later, the group comes for Silvio to smuggle him to Brazil. Norma, meanwhile, must go on with her life. She'll need a few days first, however, to clarify things with Luis.

PART IV

REVENGE

PART IV

THE EXCLUDED

BY LEANDRO ÁVALOS BLACHA

Recoleta

Translated by M. Cristina Lambert

Marcelo was the first person I met from the building. He was leaving Rogelio's apartment with a laptop under his arm. He almost dropped it when he saw me.

"I thought the police were done investigating."

My uniform always confused people. I showed him my patch: SECURITY. "I'm Rogelio's sister." I let him know I'd be moving in the next couple of days. Actually, I'd only brought a few clothes in a bag. I kept my eyes on the laptop.

"He was going to buy another one, he'd promised this one to me," he explained. "If you want it . . ."

I told him I did, that I wanted to check it just in case there was any useful information.

"The police already saw it."

"If my brother wanted to give it to you, you can have it afterward." I asked him for the keys. I'd learned to recognize a thief from my job. And I was facing one. The way they looked, moved, stood, gave them away. Marcelo didn't hide his anger.

"Welcome to the building," he said drily, and ran down the stairs.

I removed the tape marking the crime scene. There was a lot to do, beginning with changing the locks and straightening up. All of Rogelio's meticulousness had been destroyed.

They'd turned his place upside down. I saw pieces of glass and ceramic and I pictured those vases and statues on the shelves, now thrown on the floor. Whoever killed him acted viciously. The bag on his head, the cuts. It was my first time visiting the apartment. I couldn't bring myself to look around. Rogelio hadn't been talking to us. Nor were we speaking to him. We envied him.

I settled in the kitchen. I was sure I'd find a good bottle of champagne in the refrigerator. I drank almost the whole thing in one gulp, then opened another. Finally, I owned something. I couldn't help laughing. What would my brother say about that intrusion? The half-breed drinking out of the bottle a few yards from the chalk outline where they'd found his body.

The doorbell woke me up the next morning. I put on Rogelio's bathrobe—I'd never felt anything so soft. It was a very fine zebra-print silk. The bags under my eyes were dragging on the floor.

"I have to stop drinking," I said aloud, as I did every day. I tried to fix my hair.

When I opened the door I saw Marcelo. There were others behind him.

"We live in the building. We wanted to give you our condolences and deliver this." One by one they passed a silver urn around, which the super eventually handed to me.

"I'm so sorry."

"It's God's will."

"May the Lord keep him in His glory."

"He was a good man."

"We're here for whatever you need."

I stared at the urn until they left. I didn't have the slightest idea what to do with Rogelio's ashes.

I picked up the paper, La Nación, by the door. When I
returned, the place had come alive. You could hear music
in the background. The TV was turned to a news channel.
The blinds were open. The coffee maker on. I'd seen several
remote controls lying around. I'd have to figure out how to
program them. I was grateful for the coffee. It was just what
I needed.

Rogelio's death took up a full column in the newspaper's
crime pages. The news avoided the bloodier details we'd read
in Crónica when the crime occurred. They linked it to other
cases, but still didn't give details. It wasn't unusual for a thief
to claim he was a cabbie so he could rob an old fag. As no
one from the family was pushing the investigation, the police
didn't try very hard. Marcelo gave them the description of a
young guy who used to visit my brother. They had an Identi-Kit.
The only clue—sex ruined people. They'd obsess about the
security of their homes, yet would take anybody to bed.

I put the urn away in my bag, donned my uniform, and left
for work. I considered tossing the ashes in the first garbage can.
I felt guilty. Rogelio was saving me from having to commute
from Lanús. It was still strange for me. I felt like an intruder
living here. Recoleta was a bubble. We half-breeds would
come in to do our work, and then leave. Everything was too
perfect, pretty. A little Europe. I saw an imposing building and
wondered what it was. Perhaps just a school. But it looked like
a cathedral. Even death was pretty and fancy in the neighborhood. Rogelio's soul of a diva would have dreamed about a
place in the Recoleta Cemetery, among the illustrious dead.
There was no site without history or an important function:
museums, libraries, embassies, good restaurants, designer shops.
The streets smelled of imported perfumes. The old geezers
weren't abandoned and dressed in rags like in Lanús. They

strolled around looking nice—calmly, slowly, aided by their maids. Three or four of those old men might own half of Argentina. They wouldn't have lasted two minutes in Lanús. *Don't be prejudiced or resentful*, I had to repeat to myself. I felt at any moment they'd send me back to the periphery.

Before I realized it, I was at the shop.

"Good morning, Noelia," said the owner. She never called me by my name. She sounded cordial. "How're you doing?"

I shrugged. "It's life, ma'am, thank you."

She said I was right to take it like that, a good philosophy. I nodded and stood by the door looking out at the street. I checked my watch. I'd memorized the Alvear Avenue routines. The movements of the hotel tourist contingents. The time of day when some women passed by wearing sports clothes on their way to work out. Good asses, nice tits. People walking their dogs. Except for the maids, I felt I was the only one working.

Suddenly, there was a commotion in the shop. Some actresses would be coming in to try on dresses. They gave the owner prestige, but you had to squeeze them to get a cent out of them. They wanted everything for free. The owner dressed some of them for life. As for me, I usually assumed they were assholes. She'd charge them for dresses I wouldn't even wear as a whore as if they were made of golden threads. The women were delighted. I wouldn't express an opinion or say a word, even if they chatted me up. I just made sure they didn't take anything. It was surprising how quick they were at stealing.

When things quieted down, the owner asked me about the funeral. If I was a believer. If I went to Mass. I said yes to everything. It'd look bad to admit that no one from the family came. For the first time in fifteen years I dared to ask for her advice—what to do about the ashes.

"Did your brother want to be cremated?"

I nodded.

She told me she didn't approve of cremation, and even less of sprinkling the remains somewhere. She recommended I keep them or consult a parish priest. I could take them to a church cinerary.

I'd just gotten home from work when the bell rang. It was two of the neighbors.

"Gabriel, from the fourth floor."

"And I'm Olivia, my dear, from the eighth."

I vaguely recognized them.

"We know what a mess the apartment was left in; you must need help cleaning it up."

Although I'd rather have had some wine by myself, it wasn't a bad idea. I let them in and pointed to the furniture strewn about.

"I don't understand how nobody heard anything."

"Two deaf old people live upstairs and downstairs," Olivia responded.

"The one downstairs is my ex-wife," the man said.

I was surprised the fag would mention a wife.

"How dreadful. Rogelio kept this place so nice . . ."

"Did he have visitors?"

"All the time."

After a few minutes of them helping me, I ended up working by myself. Olivia had sat down and Gabriel soon joined her. They were sniffing around among Rogelio's belongings more than cleaning up.

"Is there anything of his you'd like?"

I saw their eyes brighten; they couldn't wait to get started. Gabriel went directly to the closet and took out some clothes.

Shirts and loud jackets. Olivia grabbed some knickknacks. I suspected they were expensive, but they looked hideous to me. Later they split some books between them.

"I lent him these," said the old woman. She was lying. But they came around, and went back to cleaning up. They told me about the building: The old man on the seventh floor was curt but respectful. Gabriel's ex, "a mad old woman." Two older couples lived on the lower floors. The one on the third floor never left home; he was under house arrest. Olivia said he was in the military.

"He's no longer the only law representative," she added, pointing to my security credential. "Isn't that true, Lieutenant Rodríguez?" Then she changed the subject. She'd skip from one thing to another, inserting some English words here and there. From films to astrology, from my uniform to questions about my family. For some reason, she always mentioned Marcelo.

"Ask him whatever you want, he'll take care of everything. He runs the building. He'll get you maids, nurses, pay taxes, make repairs, take care of your shopping."

Gabriel nodded. It was clear Marcelo had them eating out of his hand. He knew how to manipulate these old jerks.

Olivia didn't stop helping herself. She drank more than me. She only got up when Gabriel screamed like a lunatic when he saw the time.

The apartment actually did look a little more presentable. Someday I'd have to figure out what to do with so much space.

Olivia offered to help me decorate. "You have to give it your personal touch."

It was difficult to erase Rogelio from the place. His queerness was present in everything, from hundreds of tiny ornaments to a huge portrait on the living room wall. He came off as conceited, a show-off, young, like he had been when some rich old guy took him away from home. I laid down on the bed with his computer. I checked his Facebook updates. I couldn't resist looking at my cousin's vacation pictures. She was on the beach, in the Caribbean, with her disgusting husband Raúl, who looked like an overweight gorilla—fat, hairy, and wearing a G-string. She, with her tits about to jump out of her bikini. Too much woman for a truck driver. I moved quickly to landscape photos. I searched for another one of her in a bathing suit, and remembered our summer vacations in San Clemente. Then I went to get some wine. I could look at her for hours. But when I came back, the screen was black. I thought it must be the battery. I pushed the computer aside and looked for the cord. Suddenly, white letters appeared on the screen, like in a chat room: *Hi, Noelia.*

I tried to turn off the machine, but the text continued to appear: *We're friends of your brother's.*

I stared at the screen without responding.

And yours. Don't be afraid.

Tomorrow, after work.

Quintana and Ortiz, in front of La Biela.

In the phone booth you'll be told how to proceed.

Don't talk to anyone.

I closed the computer and ran to look out the windows. There were no people on the street. But I imagined that in the apartments across the street someone was checking me out.

Don't be crazy, Noelia, I said to myself. I looked out through the peephole. The hallway was empty. I made sure the door was locked. I stuck the computer in a cabinet and opened a bottle of wine and drank sitting in an armchair until I fell asleep.

* * *

"Goodbye, lieutenant," I heard as I was leaving. Olivia was sitting on Marcelo's stool. The boy was polishing the door a few yards away. He was wearing a tight, sleeveless T-shirt. I said hello to the woman and approached Marcelo.

"Don't you ever take off your uniform?" he asked, smiling. He'd stood up and flexed his muscles. My head was splitting.

"Why do you care?" I spat out before quickly apologizing. I had to control my reactions.

Marcelo continued to clean as I asked him about my brother, his friends, and the people who visited him.

"I don't get involved in the tenants' lives. I already told the police what little I know." He noticed I was uneasy. "Did something happen?"

But I just didn't trust him enough to be honest. "I had a strange feeling, something I didn't understand. Don't worry, thanks."

I said goodbye to Olivia and she gave me a military salute. As I walked along I noticed my bag felt heavier than usual. I was still carrying my brother's urn with me, but I didn't have time to go back and leave it in the apartment.

I rushed on to the shop and the owner arrived shortly after. She was in a bad mood, and came in without saying hello.

My mind was elsewhere all day. Shoplifters from the garment district could have come in and I wouldn't have even noticed them. The owner called me out on this once, snapping her fingers. "Wake up, dear!"

She needed help moving some furniture. Her worry in the last few days was about all the foreign brands closing their businesses in the country—less competition if they left, but their presence gave the avenue some prestige. If things continued like this, she said repeatedly, we'd soon be wearing banana peels and coconut shells, like in Venezuela.

"Did you make up your mind about your brother?"

"I'm discussing it with my parents," I lied. We didn't talk about Rogelio in our family, except for his assets.

"I hope you'll find a place for him to rest in peace."

I was the one who needed peace. I left work not knowing exactly what to do. I headed along Alvear up to Ortiz. I decided to go by La Biela and check out the scene there. It was too safe a place for anyone to try anything illicit. When I got to the tea room, I glanced around. People were strolling leisurely and accepting flyers for nearby restaurants and bars. I'd never allowed myself the pleasure of being so carefree, had never been on vacation that way. They were almost all foreigners. I approached a phone booth—it was red, like the English ones. I wondered whether the phone would ring at some point or if I'd just be waiting for nothing. I took a few steps around, pretending to be checking my cell. Then I felt something touching my bag. I quickly turned around.

"Noelia Rodríguez?" asked the man.

By then I'd grabbed him by the arm, twisting it behind his back.

"I'm the lawyer . . . don't you remember?" he said in pain.

The man had contacted me when Rogelio died, saying he could take care of the paperwork. He was my brother's age. Just as old, though more sickly. I let him go; he straightened his suit.

"Sorry. Are you all right?"

"It was my fault, being so mysterious. I didn't want to tell you anything, except in person."

He took me by the cemetery and stopped in front of an abandoned discotheque. It had a black façade, a *Closed* sign, and some half-torn posters pasted to its walls. You could see a girl's almost naked torso. The lawyer attempted to remove it.

"Some businesses are no longer welcome in the neighborhood." But he had no strength and I had to help him.

He said Rogelio had some business affairs he hadn't told me about. Investments in bars, nightclubs. Some with VIP airs like this one. They'd operated for years, but had now closed down. The neighbors harassed them.

The old man kept on walking. He didn't want to stop at any of the cafés. I was tired after standing all day at the shop.

"Rogelio had a lot of hope for you."

I burst out laughing. We'd hardly seen each other for the past thirty years.

The lawyer said I probably knew nothing about him. "But your brother was always kept abreast of everything."

I told him not to talk nonsense. We'd lived without his help, just managing to scrape by.

"He was present in every way," the lawyer insisted. Rogelio had assured him I'd be in charge of taking his place when he retired. Although he hadn't imagined a retirement like the one he had. The attorney shared his hopes. He finally asked me to sit with him in a pizzeria. He pointed to a sidewalk chair.

"Counselor," the waiter greeted him. It was quite seedy, even for me.

"He started with this."

I looked at the sign: *Rogelio Pizza.*

I turned in my resignation letter—I would stop working in just one week. It was a betrayal to the owner.

"How are . . . with everything I gave you, and at the first opportunity . . ." She muttered something about "shitty black," and added, "Don't forget to hand in your uniform."

I had no intention of doing so; I'd paid for it out of my salary. Things got worse when she saw me in church a few days later. The lawyer had shown me the one in the area, near home. I liked the place, its simplicity. Among so many huge buildings, the façade of Our Lady of Pilar was austere. I ran into the owner inside, where she was meeting with her charity group. More no-good people who came into the shop.

"You expect to leave him here?" she asked, appalled, when she saw me with the urn. She was surprised to learn that Rogelio was from the neighborhood. The old biddies looked me up and down. They couldn't imagine the ashes of a half-breed in their church. "It's a complicated procedure. Come back another day so Rosa can explain it to you; there's nobody here today."

I left with their eyes glued to my back. It looked like I was carrying a bomb.

Counselor Alterio was even more offended than I was when I told him what had happened. He must have been one of Rogelio's lovers. He spoke of him with admiration, nostalgia, affection. "Who does she think she is!"

I asked him to calm down; I'd find a better place.

"They're not worthy of him," he said.

At this point, we were meeting at the pizzeria daily to discuss Rogelio's affairs. He'd focused the shops on the rich people he hung around with. He delivered drugs to people's homes with a fleet of taxis. He would set up bars and fill them with refined whores, models, and cabaret stars. The girls from the defunct clubs now saw clients in apartments in the area. Alterio showed me how to get into Internet pages where they broadcast live.

I played dumb: "People pay for this?"

The attorney looked at me as if he knew my browser history. "There's an audience for everything."

But to pay for it, with so much free porn? Alterio told me some things weren't consumed so freely, and asked if I was open to seeing something harsher.

"I'm open to everything," I replied.

The attorney opened another browser and showed me a screen. There was a kid hanging from his wrists. He was either asleep or unconscious. Very skinny. Alterio pointed to the number of visits. "He's been like that since we grabbed him. Twenty-five days ago." In spite of his thinness, I had no problem recognizing the boy who killed my brother.

He was a spiteful boyfriend, according to Alterio. Rogelio had several romances, boys of every color, and this one had betrayed him. The attorney wanted to see him suffer. Apparently, according to the page, so did lots of people. Every so often, some hooded men would come into the room to beat or torture him.

"Isn't it better to hand him over to the police?"

Alterio gave me a look I didn't dare challenge.

"Let's go back to the paperwork." I still had to gain his trust. There were many properties, under bogus names and shell corporations. The girls lived in some of them. It wasn't clear what my role was in all of this.

"You'll find your niche," he assured me.

I accompanied him to some of the private apartments. The nearest one was in Charcas, in front of the police station. A nice block, with a school, some stupid yoga place, and a writers museum. Alterio kept the police captain happy. The girls were friendly. They were going to school and could be mistaken for any of the young women from the area. They were classy. None of the usual whores. I felt unkempt next to them. Alterio suggested I stop wearing the uniform outside work and buy some clothes. I was tempted by the idea of going back to the shop as a customer after resigning. Buying the most expensive dresses so the owner would die of rage. But the uniform gave me security. On the other hand, I could afford other luxuries. For example: having a cleaner. To find a good maid is a valuable thing. They were always talking about them at the shop, and the problems they caused. It was difficult to find a girl who understood orders, carried them out, and didn't steal. Who spoke more Spanish than Guaraní. The shop owner used to say, no matter how rich one was, she'd always depend on a half-breed to help her. Especially in sickness and old age.

I asked Marcelo to help me find a good maid. The ones I'd seen in the building were pretty. I'd run into them when they were doing errands, almost all wearing the classic uniform: black with a white collar. The military man's maid was big and strong. She seemed proud to be going into that house. Conceited. She'd never responded when I said hello.

"I just happen to have someone I can recommend," Marcelo said. I asked him to get in touch with her as soon as possible.

The shop owner's daughter had resurfaced; she was a drug addict who was nothing but trouble. She'd call the shop mad as hell to ask for money. She'd threaten her mother saying she'd tell her story to the media. She'd be hospitalized, escape, flee for a while.

"What are you looking at?" the owner asked angrily as soon as she came in, on my last day at work. She was dragging the drug addict by the hand—the girl was pale, completely out of it, anorexic, dressed like a male hooker. The shop owner was almost carrying her in her arms.

They locked themselves in the office, though we could still hear the screams. The shop was empty and I stood glued to the entrance. Not a single customer rang the bell.

After a while the owner rushed out and locked the office door behind her. The girl was banging from inside.

"Make sure nobody goes in, and that she doesn't get out of there. No matter how much she screams." She pushed me aside to get through.

"Yes ma'am."

She left mocking my last words: "Yes ma'am, yes ma'am . . . the only thing this chimpanzee can say . . ." The way that woman looked at me had affected me deeply ever since I'd gotten the job. She never doubted I was inferior in every sense. She was a rock. But the drug addict was breaking her spirit. The owner couldn't hide the fact that she'd spent the day crying. The daughter, screaming, wished the worst possible things upon her mother. For a long time, I felt the same way.

I slept in my uniform and left it on the next morning. Alterio was waiting for me in the pickup truck. We drove around the shop a few times. He knew about those things. I felt like I'd never be free of the power she had over me. When I told the lawyer what I wanted to do, he asked if I didn't think it was too much. He smiled; he was testing me.

"Rogelio wasn't mistaken about you." Alterio had been overtly resentful of the woman ever since the church episode. He was waiting for an excuse to get revenge.

The woman went through her usual routine. She arrived

at the shop with her daughter. There was a new security guard
at the entrance, a woman, frail, younger than me. Her uniform
was different, and it looked like a costume on her. There'd be
no difficulty robbing the place now. Let them find out what
the shop was like without me.

Alterio had three kids ready. We waited for the owner to
leave and the kids went in.

"Sure they won't kill anybody?" I asked Alterio. The little old man said no, but he was laughing. It was impossible
to know. Sometimes things get complicated. Two of the kids
had to overpower my replacement and the owner's assistant,
while the third took care of the girl in the office. A clean job.
No trouble. I was scared about the reaction the assisant might
have. I remembered how hysterical she'd gotten when I refused to give her my uniform.

We waited some twenty minutes in the pickup truck until
they appeared. One had his arm around the girl, like they were
lovers. The others walked behind them. We took off as soon
as they got in. They'd already given the girl some coke, and
Alterio showed her a big baggie full of it. Her eyes popped out.
One of the kids was wiping blood off his knuckles. I didn't ask.

"Cooperate and you'll win the happy box."

The girl was at her best. She'd laugh and talk nonsense. But
she performed perfectly when she had to be serious. She told
her mother she'd been kidnapped, she was all right, but she
had two hours to deliver 100,000 pesos. She repeated our instructions between sobs. The amount was pocket change for
the owner, and she could get it quickly. The last thing she
wanted was a scandal for her baby. She wouldn't report it.

The girl pounced on every baggie she was given. She was
delighted. She'd look at Alterio, fascinated.

"Take whatever you want, pretty one," he'd calm her, while promising her every other drug in the world.

We had a pretty good time talking shit about her mother. It was like a contest—who could come up with the worst insult. The girl said she was winning. I didn't contradict her to avoid causing trouble. It was easy to blame everything on a ball-busting mother. Evidently the father didn't care much, either. He had a girlfriend younger than his daughter.

"All right, baby, you're not in therapy here," I cut her off at some point.

She laughed and asked if we'd give her part of the money. Alterio offered her a job, if she wanted it. I could just see her stuck in a brothel somewhere in the middle of nowhere. He gave her another envelope. The girl kept snorting coke, and swallowed I don't know how many pills, becoming more and more of a moron. When we saw her mother at Houssay Plaza, the girl was sound asleep.

"Is she breathing?"

Alterio shrugged. In the midst of medical students, the old woman looked for the ambulance we'd told her to expect. She was supposed to open the back door and throw the bag of money inside. Then we'd free her daughter. She looked around, acted most obediently until the ambulance arrived. Just as she was about to throw the package in, two men came up behind her, shoved her inside, and closed the doors. The ambulance started moving. We kept our part of the deal and tossed the girl out next to a garbage pile. She was no longer of interest to us.

They dropped me off at home.

"Lieutenant," Olivia greeted me when I arrived. She was gossiping with Gabriel and Marcelo. Actually, they were both listening to Marcelo, fascinated. The super was gesticulating, and between gestures he'd touch his balls. I don't know what anecdote he was telling them, nor did I care. But I couldn't ignore them as I went by.

"When are we doing dinner again?" asked Olivia. "The next one's in his apartment." She pointed to Gabriel.

"Lovely. Whenever you want."

"How's the maid?" Marcelo asked.

"She's coming by tomorrow." I expressed my thanks for everything and escaped to the elevator. People who do nothing think you have nothing to do either. I smelled something bad in the elevator. I was about to accuse Marcelo of not cleaning it, when I realized the stench was coming from my own uniform.

I didn't feel comfortable with the replacement uniform. I only wore it when I had to wash the other one. I was embarrassed to welcome the maid, smelling of goat. The girl rang the bell punctually at nine and Marcelo let her up. She knocked on the door. She must have thought for sure I was retarded, because as soon as she came in I was speechless.

"My cousin told me you needed a maid," she said. I nodded. She had on a dark-blue uniform. I pointed to a chair so she could sit down. She had long, curly hair down to her waist. Dark-skinned, with short, solid legs.

I finally stammered. "Can you wash? Iron? Cook?"

She said yes to everything. She had just come from working for a family in the area. She cleaned their apartment and their country house. She took care of the children. I could picture it: pastel-colored home, a frustrated marriage, the kids spoiled in their private school uniforms. She offered to give me references, but there was no need. I explained the place belonged to my brother and what had happened. She glanced over at his portrait and crossed herself. We agreed on her pay and work hours. She could start right away and I suggested she straighten out Rogelio's clothes so I could donate them.

While she emptied the first closet I checked the computer. They were already talking on the news about an incident in Mrs. M—'s shop. They described the "brutal" beating that the assistant had taken. The daughter appeared almost dead. They blamed this on her captors, and not on the girl's addictions. The perpetual protection of the wealthy. The husband said their main concern was finding his wife . . . We had done him a great favor.

Alterio had installed a program so that I could see pages not available on regular browsers. They were still showing Rogelio's little boyfriend on one. He resisted heroically, skin and bones. I started looking at our girls' rooms and searched the address they gave: *TheRufinaExperience*. The screen was still black.

The cleaning woman, Viviana, was a blessing. Embarrassed to let her see so many bottles of alcohol, I started to drink less. She didn't wait for me to tell her what to do. She'd prepare her cleaning supplies and make her own list of chores. One morning she found the urn when she was putting away my work bag.

"What should I do with this, ma'am?" she asked.

I looked at her like a fool. I told her the truth—my indecision about the matter. How little I knew Rogelio. My suspicion of what he'd have wanted.

By now it made no difference to me whether I threw him away or kept him in the closet. But Viviana's questions about him gave me an excuse to spend some time with her outside of work. I asked her to go with me on Saturday. Viviana didn't know if she could. She had to take care of a child; she'd try. The next day she confirmed she'd come. She left my uniform clean and scented.

She arrived early on Saturday with her little boy Alberto. She apologized—there was nobody to watch him. The kid had her eyes. An intense gaze. He seemed well-mannered, quiet. But I didn't know how to talk to a child.

"Say hello to the lady," she ordered him.

The little boy gave me a kiss. I smiled like an idiot. I watched his mother as she walked to the kitchen. She was wearing jeans and a black sweater. Hair in a ponytail. Although I refused to let her work, she started making breakfast. Alterio had come over, along with the old people from the building my brother used to hang out with. Luckily, Olivia and the lawyer took care of entertaining the child.

"What's this?" he asked about the still visible chalk outline of Rogelio's body on the floor. Viviana told him to keep quiet. We hadn't been able to clean that rug or the bloodstains. He stared at the portrait and the urn in front of it. Living where he did, he must have been familiar with death.

We had some tea while they told anecdotes about my brother. He had been a complete stranger to me. I tried making up a story about a trip even I didn't believe. What I did remember wasn't pretty. I mostly stayed silent, watching Viviana. She cleared the cups when we finished, and we got ready to leave. The little boy wanted to carry the heavy urn. I could just see him tripping right away and scattering the ashes. But I put it in the bag anyway and hung it from his shoulder.

When Viviana saw him carrying it, she scolded him. "What're you doing with that? Give it back, it's not a toy."

"She gave it to me."

I played dumb and denied it. Viviana apologized.

* * *

The kid just loved the neighborhood. He was holding his mother's hand while with the other he touched the cemetery's thick brick wall. He tried to let go when he saw the McDonald's at the mall across the way.

"C'mon, Mommy," he begged. "Can we?" Then he asked me. I was going to say yes.

"Don't be rude," his mother cut him off, and they kept on walking. Olivia and Gabriel were strolling slowly, arm in arm.

Alterio came up to me. "Are you all right?"

I was feeling great. He was the one affected.

"What about the owner?"

The lawyer looked at his watch. "Buried."

"Won't there be trouble? Where is she?"

He asked me not to worry, it wasn't the time. He showed me a photo that had just arrived on his cell. You could see the woman's hands scratching the lid overhead.

The kid asked who lived in the cemetery.

"The ones who stole all the dough from this country," I replied without thinking. Some of the vaults and mausoleums were bigger than the house where I was born.

Viviana peered at me, serious. "It's a cemetery, like the one in our neighborhood," she said to her son. I wondered what about it she could compare the one in Avellaneda. I wanted to listen in on some of the guided tour groups, but Olivia said there was no need. She was familiar with the most famous graves: the dead national heroes, the Peronists, the radicals, the artists, the scientists. The gravedigger who saved up all his life to build the mausoleum where he rests today. The husband and wife with the statues depicting them back to back, the way they ignored each other in life. Alterio explained to the kid the significance of each one in Argentinian history. I was tempted to leave the ashes in front of Eva Perón's grave. Rogelio hated it when our father would take him to the brothel. Later, he liked dark guys, but not if they didn't have money. I thought about his death. A crime of passion, lustful, bloody. How many people had died at the hands of a youth who hustled them? Alterio elbowed me as we passed in front of the statue of a girl. Rufina Cambaceres. She looked like she was trying to open a door. The lawyer told us they mistook an attack of catalepsy for her death and buried her alive.

"This is art nouveau, little boy . . ." Olivia started to explain.

"Where's Alberto?" Viviana asked. We saw him in the distance chasing some cats. The mother shouted to him. She began to run after him. The old people followed her. Olivia could barely move. When I was about to join them a cat jumped on top of me. I got scared, but it wasn't trying to attack me. It rubbed against my leg. It was orange, hairy, fat. I tried to pet it. It moved away. It looked at me and hurried off faster. It moved gently among the graves.

"Come here, damnit," I called out, but the more I called, the more it ran away from me. Somehow I became obsessed with it. I followed it until it stopped to sniff a statue. *Luis Ángel Firpo (1894–1960)*. A slender bronze man, well built, in a bathrobe baring his chest. I sensed a commotion coming from one side. Little Alberto appeared, smiling, the old people behind him. He stayed next to me. Viviana shook him hard for disobeying. The old people were out of breath, but they calmed down and stared at the statue.

"What do you think?" I asked.

"He'd be delighted," Alterio maintained.

The others nodded. Even Viviana. She explained to Alberto that the man had been a famous boxer. I had no doubt Rogelio would only find the peace the owner talked about with someone like that. We kissed the urn and covered the boxer's body with my brother's ashes.

DEATH AND THE CANOE

BY CLAUDIA PIÑEIRO

San Telmo

Translated by M. Cristina Lambert

J ust a few weeks earlier, the Spanish bookstore Papiros had opened a branch in Buenos Aires, in San Telmo, in front of Dorrego Square, betting on the constant tourism in the city's southern area. There was no better way to draw attention to the opening than to invite the star writer of the day, Martín Jenner, to give a talk and sign copies of his books.

Jenner would be punctual, as was his habit. He had decided to walk, despite the fact that it would take him almost half an hour to get there from his apartment in Puerto Madero— rented for him by his publisher, after his divorce, as part of his latest fabulous contract. No other author in Argentina had ever managed such a book deal, but no other author had ever sold more than half a million copies of every work he published, no matter what kind of book it was, simply because it carried his name.

On the way, he was surprised by how dirty that part of the city was, and he was especially surprised to see the groups of boys blasting loud music, sitting in the middle of the sidewalk, drinking beer. Martín Jenner felt invisible as he walked by, unlike in many of the other Buenos Aires neighborhoods. Being ignored outraged more than surprised him.

These people don't read, he concluded as he passed in front of the statue of the comic strip character Mafalda. A woman asked him to take her picture, though not with him, of herself sitting on the bench next to the statue.

"I'm in a hurry," he said, continuing on his way.

Despite the long walk, he looked impeccable when he arrived at the bookstore. He checked his reflection in the glass door and smoothed his hair and lapel. The bookstore was already full, and that took away the unease he had felt being ignored on his walk. Indeed, surrounded by so many people who had come to see him made him feel like himself once again. The new Papiros was quite large, but the audience exceeded the organizers' expectations, and they had to add more chairs.

As soon as he went in he was welcomed by his editor—who also played the part of being a slave to all of his requests, no matter what they were—and the publishing house's business manager, who only went to presentations by their best-selling authors. The conversation would be led by the editor in chief of a widely read cultural magazine.

By the third question, it was clear that the insecure woman was trying to show off by making obscure connections between Jenner's different texts, crowning her theory with: "It's obvious there's a deep tie between them, don't you think? From the language, I mean."

"No, I don't think so," the author replied, and from that point he spoke about whatever he felt like, without passing the microphone back to her until the talk concluded.

Exactly one hour after the event started, Jenner said goodbye without taking questions from the public. He thanked everyone, received great applause, and announced he would be there awhile longer to sign copies of his books. With his usual smile, his perfectly manicured hands polished in blue, and a Lamy pen—more common among architects than writers—Jenner signed copies of *Death and the Canoe* for more than an hour. The line of readers seeking his signature, unlike with many other authors, was not limited to middle-aged women, but included fans ranging in age from twenty to sixty, and included as many men as women. The only common denominator was that they all were obviously in love with the author. Jenner had known for some time the effect he had on his readers, and encouraged it with various strategies. And he did so once again that afternoon in San Telmo's bookstore, devoting time to every one of them, celebrating all their flattery with false humility.

Martín Jenner was, without a doubt, the most widely read author in the country, and the most translated. And, he was certain, he owed more to his readers than to the critics. Or to his colleagues, who were always evasive when commenting on his work, giving reserved praise without uttering anything negative. Jenner had never been selected as a finalist for any national or local awards, nor were his novels ever chosen as "The Year's Best Fiction" at fairs or festivals or for year-end lists. Jenner would tell himself—and the few who dared ask— that he did not care: his award or prize was there, in front of him, lining up to get their book signed. That is why Jenner did not limit himself to a simple autograph. Rather, he would ask each one of his readers for their full name, and have them spell it out if necessary. He would chat with them awhile, and would pose for hundreds of cell phone photos, including selfies. Therein lay the reason, he was convinced, his readers were so loyal. And loyal not so much to what he wrote, but to *him*. Jenner made those people standing there waiting for his signature think they knew him; they were his family, there was a real bond. That was for Jenner the real engine of the author-reader contract. And although he did not care too much for that intimacy—it rather repulsed him—he kept it up because he had no doubt that it directly influenced, perhaps exponentially, his book sales. Today, as Martín Jenner had known since his first steps in the literary world, a writer does not get anywhere just by writing. And he had gotten far. Very far.

As soon as the last photo was taken, he stood up, went to the coat rack, and slipped his coat on, getting ready to go out into the misty, gray May day. Beyond the glazed door, on the cobbled street, a group of young people were kicking a bottle and shouting. It looked like they were arguing, but they were not.

Their manner of speaking, their thunderous handling of the language, thought Jenner, *they'll all go deaf very young in this neighborhood.* He watched the group head down toward Alem Avenue, dodging cars headed in the opposite direction. He wondered if they were the squatters in the abandoned public building whom for years the government had not dared evict. He quickly abandoned the thought. After all, what did he care where those people lived?

Jenner put his pen in his pocket, and finally joined his editor, the publisher's business manager, and the bookstore owner, who were waiting to take him to dinner. They would have waited as long as necessary. He was their superstar, the most successful author on the publisher's roster, the one who made up for the losses incurred from publishing better literature.

And they were about to leave when the door was thrust open. A thin, rather untidy man maybe in his early thirties—difficult to tell with his hipster beard—approached them. He carried a backpack, from which he removed a copy of *Death and the Canoe*. The bookstore owner waylaid him.

"Excuse me, the signing's over. If you like, you can leave your copy and pick it up in a few days."

The man did not move. He looked Jenner in the eye without saying a word. The tense silence made Jenner uneasy and he felt the need to break it.

"Please," Jenner protested. "Of course I'll sign it, it'll only take a minute." He reached into his pocket and removed his pen.

The man handed him the book. As usual, Jenner opened it to the first page, ready to sign. But something confused him. Instead of the title page, he found a glued, lined piece of paper, torn from a notebook. He looked up at the man as if asking permission to remove it.

"Read," the man told him.

Jenner obeyed, but what he read he did not say aloud. *I wrote this book, Mr. Jenner, and you know it. Swine. Swindler.*

Martín Jenner turned pale, his legs shook. At first he considered saying something, or even having the man thrown out by the security guard standing by the door. But almost immediately, as soon as he could control the shaking of his legs, he concluded the best thing to do was to pretend he had not read the message. So, without looking at the bearded hipster, he signed the book and gave it back to him, barely touching the note. Although Jenner avoided eye contact, the man continued to stare at him as he put his copy back in his bag and left without a word.

"What a strange guy! There are such characters in this city," said the editor, who had not noticed anything other than the rather snooty attitude of the man with the backpack.

"Yes, it's true," Jenner responded. He thought it best not to mention the note or the insult. At least for now.

As they walked to the restaurant, Jenner stumbled over San Telmo's damp, cobbled streets, feeling a lingering discomfort in his chest. Only a few hours earlier, he had walked from his house on these same streets, with the same humidity and the same shoes, yet he did not remember having such difficulty. But it was darker now, and there was more garbage to dodge on the streets. San Telmo was always invaded by garbage at night.

They had made reservations at a classic, yet fashionable Basque restaurant not far from the bookstore that was considered one of the top ten restaurants in the city. At the entrance, after the hostess greeted them, the business manager informed Jenner that it had not been easy to get a table, but since they knew it was his favorite restaurant, they had moved heaven and earth.

Dinner was uneventful. But it was the calm before the storm, apparently, because as they walked back toward their car parked at Dorrego Square, they again encountered the man with the hipster beard. Martín Jenner recognized him immediately, dodged him, and quickened his step. Only because of this change of pace did the others notice what was happening. They all quickly got inside the editor's car.

The bearded man approached the vehicle and stood next to the front windshield. He raised the windshield wiper, then lowered it, leaving under it a sheet of notebook paper, similar to the one inside the book Jenner had signed. Jenner guessed what was likely written on it. The man stood there awhile longer, looking him directly in the eye, the middle finger of his right hand pointing up, with the rest of his fingers in a tight fist. "Fuck you," he snapped.

No one inside the car moved or said a word, until finally the man crossed the square diagonally and disappeared on Carlos Calvo, walking toward 9 de Julio Avenue. When he was definitely out of sight, the business manager got out of the car and removed the paper from under the windshield wiper. Jenner would have liked to stop him, but he knew it would have been in vain.

The business manager got back in the car and read the note: "*I wrote* Death and the Canoe. *You're an impostor, Mr. Jenner, a swine, a swindler.*"

"For God's sake!" said the editor.

"Unbelievable," said the bookseller. The car was invaded by an uncomfortable silence.

"I wonder who that madman is. Did his face look familiar to anyone?" the business manager finally asked.

Jenner moved his hands in the air, looking for words he could not find, before saying he did not have the slightest idea who the man was. The bookstore was the first time he'd ever seen the man. And then he did tell them about the note in the book he'd signed.

"Why didn't you say anything before?" the editor asked. "This man's in very bad shape. It's not the first time I've seen something like this. There are many people in this city who have the delusion that they're writers, and that a famous author stole their masterpiece."

"In this city, there are more people who write than people who read," complained the business manager.

"But usually they just denounce you in a newspaper, or they sue you, and that's that," said the editor.

"In those cases we easily resolve it with our lawyers. But this type of harassment is dangerous. Don't you think we should report it to the police?" suggested the business manager.

"I think so," said the bookseller. "We can go now, there's a precinct nearby."

Jenner, still pale from the scare, tried to keep both himself and the group calm. "Let me think for a moment; let's wait a little while longer. Nothing like this has ever happened to me before. But I've had people waiting for days to give me a book written by them, or to ask for an autograph, or even to give me a red rose. Oh well, there are always strange, intense people who get obsessed with you. But usually they get over it. It'll happen to this guy too."

"You want me to chase him away, say something to him? Just to scare him a little, so we don't have to worry it'll happen again?" asked the business manager.

"No, no, it's not worth it. Besides, he must have already gotten on a bus or a subway by now," replied Jenner. "Better not to pay him any attention. They all seek a little fame at someone else's expense. And once they have their minute of glory, they're all right."

They took off, ending their exchange of ideas, but during the drive they continued talking about the man with the hipster beard. The business manager dropped off the bookstore owner at his house a few blocks away. He lived on Defensa, but in an area where this street in San Telmo begins to lose its charm and turns into the city's business district, a place which at night, without the city's hustle and bustle, frightens many. Then they continued to Puerto Madero to drop off Martín Jenner.

"Sure you're all right?" the editor asked.

"Of course I am," said Jenner. "All I need is to lose my cool over some deluded hipster who believes he wrote what I wrote. Don't worry, it's no more than an anecdote we'll tell at a company toast until we get tired of it." Jenner shook the business manager's hand, kissed the editor on the cheek, and got out, but before heading into his apartment, he turned back and approached the car window to say one last thing. "Obviously, this is going to cost you a few extra dollars on the next contract; unhealthy work, friend," he warned, and everyone laughed, although they knew that when it came to Jenner, this was not a joke.

The business manager waited before driving off because his best-selling writer was not going inside the building. Jenner searched his pockets for his keys, but before finding them, the building's security guard approached and let him in. Jenner lifted his hand and waved goodbye. The others tooted the horn and drove away.

While Martín Jenner was walking toward the elevator, the security guard approached him again and gave him a pile of mail. He told Jenner that he himself had taken it out of the mailbox because there was no more room inside.

Jenner took it and thanked him for his trouble. "I'm hopeless when it comes to mailboxes," he remarked as he stepped into the elevator.

Inside the apartment, he threw the envelopes on the coffee table, took off his shoes, and poured himself a glass of whiskey, aimlessly playing with the ice cubes in the glass while he relaxed into an armchair. He glanced over at the scattered envelopes on the coffee table, and one of them caught his attention. The address showed his name, but underneath, in parentheses, it read: *SWINE, SWINDLER*. He would have liked to simply relax, but this was too much. Trembling, he opened it and found what he'd suspected: a letter from the man with the hipster beard, who had finally identified himself as Antonio Borda. He reminded Jenner that he had mailed him three copies of his manuscript, *Death and the Canoe*, last year: one in March, one in August, and the last one in October.

As I told you in my last letter, they were the only three copies I had, and I sent them to you without reservation because I trusted you. You told me at the bookfair that

you'd love to read what I wrote. Or don't you remember?
Or do you tell everybody that?

Of course I tell everybody that, Jenner thought, and continued to read. In the remainder of the letter, Borda thanked him for reading the manuscripts, and then went on in three long paragraphs about the virtue of his own text, *which I realize now you also valued.* Finally, he ended the letter with a paragraph Jenner felt to be threatening:

> *I won't contact you again, but if you don't declare publicly*
> *that I'm the author of* Death and the Canoe *in the next*
> *seventy-two hours, I will commit suicide, and you will*
> *carry that burden for the rest of your life.*

Martín Jenner felt like he was going to faint. He was very upset by this madman and needed to talk to someone. He dialed his editor's number, but quickly hung up. It would be better to tell her about it the next day. Why make someone else lose a night's sleep? Perhaps he would call his lawyer directly, he thought. In any case, he was not afraid the man would kill himself. *They say that truly suicidal people do it without warning,* he remembered. And Borda had said seventy-two hours. No one plans a suicide for three days later. Jenner was sure of that. *The hipster must be looking for money,* he concluded. *If he knows anything else about me, the most successful writer in Argentina, he won't get it. Enough,* he told himself. And after a third whiskey, he took a sleeping pill.

Three days later, Antonio Borda's body was found hanging in front of the Papiros bookstore. The Dorrego Square storekeepers surrounded the body, which hadn't yet been authorized for removal. Borda had, in his pocket, a letter addressed to the bookstore, which had said more or less the same thing in the letter he sent to Martín Jenner.

The incident turned into a scandal that was covered by all the media. They spent weeks talking about the suicide, alternating between referring to Borda as a *hipster*, *compulsive liar*, or *poet*.

Martín Jenner testified before the courts, and soon after, an extensive story aired about him on one of the most popular prime-time news programs, where it was unusual to see a novelist appearing as a guest. "I didn't consider how badly that young man was doing. I feel guilty. He needed help, and I didn't see it. Sometimes it happens that someone has an idea that another writer actually develops, and he feels cheated. It happens all the time. Coincidences, topics that are in the air and take different literary forms in writers' imaginations. Ah well, I think that in his delusion he must have been convinced that he sent me his manuscript and that I wrote something that belonged to him. Delusion has strange, indescribable paths, even for us writers. It's too bad no one noticed what bad shape he was in."

In closing, Martín Jenner said: "I'm an agnostic, but if I weren't, I'd ask for a prayer for him." There was a moment of silence, and then the news program completed their story with a report from an important mental illness specialist.

The hipster had a record of psychological disorders, had been hospitalized twice, and the only family member who had come to identify the body was a distant aunt who had not seen him in years.

Eventually, though, some new scandal emerged and the media coverage waned. A few weeks later, *Death and the Canoe* went into its twenty-first printing.

* * *

"Well, I don't want to be morbid, but in the end the hipster did us a favor," the editor told Martín Jenner when she called to let him know about the new printing.

"I don't find that funny, but I'm happy about the new edition," replied Jenner.

Then they went over details about his upcoming participation in the Paraty literary festival in Brazil. His editor tried to get him excited, reminding him it was "an event very few attend," as if Jenner were not quite clear which festival it was.

For years it had bothered him each time the guest list appeared and he was not on it. "Yes, I suppose we'll say yes to the Paraty people. Let me think about it for a little while, though," he said, and then hung up.

Jenner went to the window. The river was grayer than usual. Far off he could see a ship, so small in the distance that it looked like a canoe. He felt like pouring himself a drink, but if he started this early in the morning, he would not be able to write for the rest of the day, so he ruled it out. It was better to start writing now on his laptop, in front of the window that provided such a unique perspective. But before that, he went to his desk to finally do what he had avoided until now. Perhaps out of superstition? Out of respect for the dead? Out of delight? Savoring a risk that at one time he feared could break him? He did not know why he waited until now, but it was time. From the bottom drawer, he removed the three copies of Borda's manuscript he had received in the mail, in March, August, and October of last year. He set them on fire in the kitchen sink, waiting until they burned. He carefully gathered the ashes in a vase. He put a dish over it, just in case. And he placed the vase in the living room library. They would remain there until he had time to go down to the banks of that river he could see from his window. When he went to the river, he swore to himself, he would scatter them. *I hope,* he thought, *that at that very moment a canoe goes by and the ashes fly in front of it, like the ashes of a cremated body.*

FEEL THE BURN

BY MARÍA INÉS KRIMER

Monte Castro

Translated by M. Cristina Lambert

arcia buys candles at Lascano's Chinese shop. As she leaves, the neon illuminates her face with a play of light and shadow. Garbage containers. Damp papers. Empty bottles. Tins. Since the power outages started, neighbors have been burning tires on the avenue. There's a fuel shortage. Lines of cars waiting to fill their tanks.

A policeman standing at the entrance of a bare brick building plays with a cell phone. Marcia stops for a moment at the corner of Segurola, looks at him, dodges a loose tile, goes on. She can't put her finger on exactly what she's looking for on the poorly lit sidewalks, on the nocturnal faces she comes across in the streets.

The insomnia that resulted from her separation from Pablo has forced her to walk one, two hours after dinner: her strategy has been to roam until she gets tired. It was on one of those rounds that she noticed a green-lettered sign that says, *Cross Fire*. The gym is on the second floor, in the middle of the block. A door with bars. An ad for an energy drink. The picture of a muscular athlete behind glass. Marcia didn't hesitate to spend her last savings on Nike leggings and Air Jordan sneakers. She has been going to the gym three times a week ever since she moved to Monte Castro.

Marcia climbs the stairs. The room with treadmills, stationary bikes, and rowing machines is in front. To one side, a bar with Formica tables and croissants under a bell jar. The girl at the desk takes the gum out of her mouth, stretches it, and reinserts it. She fans herself with a flyer. "Hot," she says.

"Deadly," Marcia replies. A black cat jumps out of the dark and lands next to her leg as she goes into the aerobics room. A cracked mirror covers part of the wall. Humidity is seeping in through the baseboards. The class that night has more people than usual because the power outages forced several cancellations last month. Marcia picks up a mat, places it near the window. A woman with fluorescent nails stretches her arms on the barre, swings her head from one side to the other. She stands up and settles near the platform. A tough-looking guy in shorts and a fuchsia top comes in at the last minute and stands in the front row.

The instructor hangs a toy skeleton near the mirror. "Come on, we don't have all night. Grab some dumbbells and go up to the barre."

The fan blades whirl. Shakira floods the aerobics room.

"Jog."

Marcia beats the tough guy and the woman with fluorescent nails by a few yards. Despite the loud music, she can hear car horns on the street, sneakers rubbing, keys jangling inside a fanny pack. The click of Pablo's lighter rings in her head the whole time. They're on the second set of reps when Shakira falls silent. The instructor touches the tray, taps it with his finger. He takes out the CD, examines it on both sides. Puts it back in. He waits a few seconds. "It's had it," he says. There's a moment's hesitation, no one knows whether to continue or not, until they hear: "Dumbbells."

The instructor grabs a five-pound set and, back turned, explains that biceps must be worked with extra weight to achieve a lasting effect. The students do four sets of twenty reps each. Marcia can't stop looking at the tough guy; she's surprised at how well he has coordinated his shorts with his top. The only sound in the room now is measured breathing, arms moving up and down, the buzzing of the fan blades. The relative silence amplifies the noise coming from outside.

"Barre."

Marcia grasps the barre with her hands, her wrists aligned. Her spine straight. Her elbows glued to her body: if she bends forward or moves sideways, other muscles will be used. Suddenly the lights go out.

"Another power failure," someone says.

The instructor turns on a flashlight. "We go on," he says, and tilts the beam downward. "On the floor." Now the skeleton is no longer white but yellow. Marcia stretches her arm until she touches the mat. She looks at the desert of bodies scattered throughout the room. A smell of burned tires comes through the window. She remembers the bonfires of her childhood, the firewood piled in the middle of the street. At first the fire was slow, then more intense, and later it would rise, driven by the wind.

"Abs."

Marcia corrects her posture: head relaxed, chin separated from her body. She runs a finger over her belly. *The routine's having an effect*, she thinks. There are sighs, complaints, desertions. The woman's fluorescent nails search for a bottle of mineral water.

The instructor says: "Feel the burn."

Someone approaches, groping in the dark until she finds an empty mat. Marcia smells something thick, acid. She then hears a long sigh, as if the new arrival has come a long way and it's hard to find a place in the room.

"I'm paid up through the end of the year," the woman explains as she settles on the cheap leather.

The instructor presses: "Feel the burn."

Marcia thinks about the cop standing at the bare brick building. She was awakened two nights ago by the siren of an ambulance. After that she had a hard time getting back to sleep, and when she finally did, at dawn, she dreamed about the crackling of flames, heat, the house opening its mouth, gasping for air. Every once in a while a flash would burst out in another area, and the firefighters' hoses would turn toward the windows while sparks flew and a thick column of smoke climbed up to the sky.

"It hurts," a voice said.

"What?"

"My skin, when it burns."

Marcia wonders whether that voice was announcing what's ahead for her—that she'd end up talking with a stranger in some dump of a gym. When she moved to Monte Castro, after the separation, she stopped seeing her friends. No one was going to cross the city to have coffee or share a happy hour at the Álvarez Jonte tea room, among retirees playing cards, cabbies discussing a soccer game, and women just leaving the hairdresser's.

"You moved to the boonies," they reproached her.

"Cheap rent," Marcia responded. She was ashamed to tell them Pablo's threats forced her to look for someplace far away. She doesn't want to think about the click of the yellow lighter or the cell phone smashed on the floor or the long sleeves she wore all summer to cover the bruises on her arms.

"Glutes."

Marcia turns, gets down on all fours, and lifts her right leg until she forms a right angle. She looks to her side.

The woman on the mat is wiping sweat from her forehead with the palm of her hand. "I can't take it anymore," she says. When she stands up, the beam from the flashlight illuminates a dark ear, like a charred fig.

Marcia attempts to follow the routine, but realizes she can't. She's under the impression that the ear is another warning. She closes her eyes not to see flames. The heat burns just the same. The door is ajar and the silence is broken by the instructor's voice and the faint street sounds. The moment the figure disappears on the stairs, the power comes back. There's clapping, shouts of excitement. The woman with fluorescent nails opens the water bottle and takes a sip. The tough guy adjusts his shorts in the mirror. Marcia stares at the empty mat. There's a strip of yellow and sticky gauze on the mat.

As she's leaving she trips over the little skeleton. It's now completely dark outside. In the distance, she sees the flash of tires on the avenue. A woman with supermarket bags. A man walking a poodle. The dog crosses in front of her and growls. She feels her legs soaked under the leggings. When she reaches the corner of Segurola, she stops at the brick building.

"Something happen?"

The cop looks up from the screen of his cell phone. "A man dumped alcohol on his wife," he says. "Then he set her on fire. The neighbors heard the screams."

"How is she?"

The cop doesn't answer.

Marcia quickens her pace. When she turns onto Lascano, she stops. She removes a damp newspaper from the trash, then buries it deeper in the bin. She wipes her fingers on her leggings.

Her hand is shaking as she opens the elevator door. *What if Pablo finds out where I live?* she thinks. She puts the key in the lock. She's surprised there's a light on inside. She forgot to turn it off because of the power outage.

ABOUT THE CONTRIBUTORS

VERÓNICA ABDALA was born in Buenos Aires in 1973. She currently works as a journalist in the culture section of the Argentinian newspaper *Clarín* and has published articles on culture and literature in the other newspapers as well, including *La Nación* and *Página/12*. She is the author of the illustrated biography *Borges for Beginners* and the essay "Susan Sontag and the Office of Thinking."

DaríoRomero

LEANDRO ÁVALOS BLACHA was born in Quilmes, Argentina, in 1980. In 2007, he won the Indio Rico prize for his novel *Berazachussetts*, selected by the writers César Aira, Alan Pauls, and Daniel Link. He is also the author of *Serialismo*, *Medianera*, and *Malicia*.

Marcos Brindicci

GABRIELA CABEZÓN CÁMARA was born in Buenos Aires, and is the author of *La Virgen Cabeza, Le viste la cara a Dios, Beya, le viste la cara a Dios, Romance de la Negra Rubia, Sacrificios,* and *Y su despojo fue una muchedumbre.*

Hartwig Klappert

INÉS GARLAND was born in Buenos Aires and still lives there. She has published several novels and short story collections. Her second novel, *Piedra, papel o tijera*, was selected by ALIJA—a children's and young adult literary association—as the best novel of the year. It has been translated into German, French, Italian, and Dutch. With this novel, Garland was the first Spanish-speaking writer to win the prestigious German children's book prize, Deutscher Jugendliteraturpreis.

M. CRISTINA LAMBERT was born in Córdoba, Argentina, and moved to New York City as a teenager. She is the translator of *Looking at Photographs*, for the New York Museum of Modern Art, and a historical novel, *Una sombra donde sueña Camila O'Gorman (A Shadow Where Camila O'Gorman Dreams)*, by the Argentinian surrealist poet Enrique Molina. Several of her translated short stories have appeared in *Beacons*, the literary magazine of the American Translators Association.

MARÍA INÉS KRIMER was born in 1951 in Paraná, Argentina, and now resides in Buenos Aires. She is the author of *Veterana*, *La hija de Singer* (winner of the Premio del Fondo Nacional de las Artes), *El cuerpo de las chicas*, *Lo que nosotras sabíamos* (winner of the Emecé Prize), *Sangre kosher*, *La inauguración* (winner of a Letra Sur Prize), and *Siliconas express*. Most recently, Krimer published *Sangre Fashion*, the third book in the Ruth Epelbaum detective series.

Maximiliano Luna

ARIEL MAGNUS was born in Buenos Aires in 1975 and has published fifteen books, mostly novels. The third one, *Un Chino en bicicleta*, published in 2007, won the La otra orilla prize—with César Aira as head of the jury—and was translated into six languages. He works as a literary translator of German, English, and Portuguese.

Leandro Teysseire

ERNESTO MALLO is an Argentinian journalist, screenwriter, playwright, and novelist, and also the organizer of BAN! Buenos Aires Negra, an international noir book festival. In addition to plays and scripts, he has published ten prize-winning novels that have been translated into seventeen different languages. He is a former active member of the resistance to the military rulers of the sixties and seventies. Mallo lives and works in Buenos Aires, Argentina, and Barcelona, Spain.

Ocelote

ENZO MAQUEIRA was born in Buenos Aires in 1977. He is the author of *Historias de Putas*, *Ruda macho*, *El Impostor*, and the critically acclaimed novel *Electrónica*.

Ana Inés Bagni

INÉS FERNÁNDEZ MORENO was born in Buenos Aires. She has worked as a creative director at several advertising agencies and has written extensively for newspapers and magazines. Her most recent novel, *El cielo no existe*, was awarded the 2014 Sor Juana Inés de la Cruz Prize, which recognizes female authors who write in Spanish. Her most recent work is a collection of short stories, *Malos Sentimientos*.

ELSA OSORIO was born in Buenos Aires. A novelist and scriptwriter, her work has been translated into twenty languages. Her novel *A veinte años, Luz* is considered a classic of Latin American literature. Her other novels include *Cielo de Tango, Callejón con salida,* and *Mika, La capitana.* She was awarded a Chevalier de l'Orde des Arts et des Lettres from the French government for her contributions to literature and human rights, among other prizes.

ALEJANDRO PARISI was born in Buenos Aires in 1976. He has published six novels: *Delivery, El ghetto de las ocho puertas, Un caballero en el purgatorio, La niña y su doble, Con la sangre en el ojo,* and *Su rostro en el tiempo.* Several of his books have been published in different languages, including French and Italian.

CLAUDIA PIÑEIRO, a novelist and screenwriter, was born in Buenos Aires in 1960. She has won numerous literary prizes, among them the German LiBeraturpreis for *Elena Sabe* and the Sor Juana Inés de la Cruz Prize for *Las grietas de Jara.* Her other published works include *Un comunista en calzoncillos, Betibú, Tuya,* and *Las viudas de los jueves.*

PABLO DE SANTIS was born in Buenos Aires in 1963, and is the author of the novels *The Paris Enigma* and *Voltaire's Caligrapher,* published in English by HarperCollins. He has also written a number of books for young adults, including *El inventor de juegos,* adapted into the film *The Games Maker.* His graphic novel *El hipnotizador,* illustrated by Juan Sáenz Valiente, became a TV series and premiered on HBO Latinoamérica in 2015.

ALEJANDRO SOIFER was born in Buenos Aires in 1983. He earned a bachelor's degree in comparative literature, with majors in Spanish teaching and Latin American and Argentinian literature at the University of Buenos Aires. He has published two crime-fiction novels, *Rituales de sangre* and *Rituales de lágrimas.* He is currently completing an MA in Hispanic Studies at the University of Toronto in Canada.

 **JOHN WASHINGTON** is a freelance journalist and translator. He is a frequent contributor to the *Nation,* where he writes about immigration and criminal justice. He has translated numerous books, including *The Beast* and *The Story of Vicente, Who Murdered His Mother, His Father, and His Sister: Life and Death in Juárez,* both published by Verso Books.